# T OF LIVING BETTER

Here's what They don't tell you about living an Optimal Life.

*A novel by*

## ELLIOT BARNETT

My Core Insights, LLC
Forest Grove, Oregon

# THE MYTH OF LIVING BETTER
By Elliot Barnett

The information contained in this book is intended to be entertaining and educational, and not for diagnosis, prescription, or treatment of any health disorder. This information should not replace consultation with a healthcare professional. The author and publisher are in no way liable for any misuse of the material.

Published by My Core Insights, LLC,
Forest Grove, Oregon • www.mycoreinsights.com

International Standard Book Number: 979-8-9854320-1-5


Printed in the United States of America

*Cover design by CANDesigner*

Dedicated to my wife
for her devotion and undying support,

to my family for believing in me,

and to those who have chosen to take their journey to
living their Optimal Life.

You can be more than you were. What was simply was. What will be is up to you. Your moment holds an eternity within for you to realize your Optimal Life.

-Elliot Barnett

# CONTENTS

# BREAKING FREE

Jeremy's eyes opened as his lungs gasped for air. The intensity seemed to increase each morning as the distance lengthened from his last drink of noggy.

He loved the rebellious instinct that drove him to stop drinking that foul-tasting substance that seemed to sustain everyone else in his community, but he has noticed a clear consequence to his decision. Things were louder, stronger, more overwhelming.

He laid there still, staring at the ceiling, trying to sort through the new sensations and thoughts that emerged from an impossibly opaque place within him. He felt more awake at that moment than, well, he had ever felt. All these unfamiliar words revealed themselves. He felt sensations he hadn't before. It was an awareness—

"Where the goddamn hell are those keys!" his mother yelled from the hallway outside Jeremy's room. "You're still in bed? Why are you lying there? You're going to be late. Every single morning you get up later than you should, make me late, and make yourself late...and upset everyone around you."

Another outburst—well, THAT certainly was familiar! His mother's outbursts were enough to shake anyone out of this introspection that was so unfamiliar to him. His mother always seemed to be in this frantic, irate state of accusations and attack.

*What a ridiculous woman. She drives me crazy and makes*

*me so mad*, he thought.

"Well, if you put the damn things in the same place, you wouldn't be running around looking for them, now would you?" Jeremy snapped back.

What does Jeremy staying in bed have to do with her leaving? Nothing! He rides his bike to class. She just loves complaining and giving him a hard time. It's what she lives for. It's what all Reactors live for.

He propelled himself out of bed and into the hall. That new feeling, now almost constantly present within him, became louder and heightened in a way. He felt sick to his stomach. His anxiety was overwhelming and seemed worse in these moments. Maybe if his mother would stop, that gnawing feeling within him would slow this attack. He had the urge to deny his rebellion and seek a little relief by downing a glass of that thick grayish substance, but it would defy his stubborn nature and give an opening to his mother he would just prefer to deny her.

Jeremy shook his head while he watched his mother's crooked body race past his father walking by. His father had the tone-deaf look that was pervasive for the Insensors in their community. Seemingly unaware of his wife's heightened emotional state, his father lumbered by with a noticeable slump in his stance, while staring blankly at Jeremy.

"Hey, old man," Jeremy said with the best sheepish tone he could muster.

His father replied with a grunt, just as Jeremy expected.

*Is this what we are aspiring to be?* Jeremy wondered. *Is this Insensor state what we want to evolve toward?*

Jeremy never questioned  anything before, but certainly not the idea that Reactors hopefully and eventually became Insensors. Is this his destiny? Is this what he's meant for? Enduring what life sends their way is what each person in the community is supposed to live for. That's what everyone is told before they even can understand what the words mean.

*God, look at how slumped over he is,* Jeremy thought while he watched his father. Jeremy could already feel the weight curving at his spine. He looked at his bag of rocks, smaller than his mother's and much smaller than his father's. His parents had a long head-start in accumulating them.

These rocks are the rewards for facing the trials in their lives. From as early as he can remember, the community's mantras echoed in his ears: "You carry the weight of your existence and bear it for all," and everyone's favorite "what was will always be." Having to drag himself to classes to hear them once again evoked his anger, which momentarily quieted his anxiety. But his thoughts returned, ushering his anxiety back to center stage.

Jeremy was thankful that he'd have time before the accumulated weight took its toll on him as it had his parents. This was near blasphemy within his community. Everyone is supposed to be eager for their fate. But, to him, it seemed he could do more, be more, but how? How can he break away from this chaotic drudgery that surrounds him? His anxiety again succumbed to his anger. He could feel it well up inside of him as if there was something within him surging with energy, directing his actions.

He kicked the kitchen door open, feeling the relief he was seeking for allowing the actions to flow from his body. Like all Reactors, he looked around frantically for another immediate action to take when his eyes locked on the tall glass of noggy on the table, waiting for him.

"Are you kidding me right now, Mom?"

This was his opportunity to fight back again. He grasped the glass so tightly that he almost shattered it and glared at his mother while he walked to the sink.

"Don't even think about it!" his mother yelled.

With a sideways glance and smirk, Jeremy poured the slop down the sink. These were the moments where his inner chaos paused where he could see his actions right through to their consequences—more verbal attacks from his mother.

"You aren't going to amount to anything," she said. "How the hell do you expect to have a chance of becoming an Insensor if you don't treat yourself the way you're supposed to! Are you that thick-headed?"

Jeremy marched by his mother with a skip in his step. His parents seemed equally absurd to him but in different ways. He might be a Reactor like his Mother, but he could feel a shift within him pushing him further away from how she lives. And his father was no one he wanted to be like, no matter what the supposed destiny was for people in his community. He held onto the feeling that he knew better than them, that he was better than them. He wanted them to see how much so, but how could they with their blind eyes and narrow gazes? There was, however, a sense of comfort in this truth.

Jeremy returned to his room to throw on the gray-on-gray clothes everyone his age wore to class.

"I don't understand why you haven't left yet," his mother said. "You failed to live on your own, so now you have to live here and listen to me. Once a failure, always a failure. The least you could do is be on time for your classes!"

"Just leave me alone!" Jeremy shot back. "It's not my fault I lost my job, it's theirs. They didn't need my help anymore so that was that! What was I supposed to do? Do you think I want to be here with the two of you? I'm an adult! And, besides, I already found another job. I just need time to save money."

"Oh, right! Like you'll do that. You tried living on your own and you failed, so that's that. What was will always be. Now, enough of your nonsense and get going. You've already made me late!"

His mother turned and walked out the door before Jeremy could attempt another defense. As if he didn't feel bad enough about losing his job and having to move back home. He wanted to save extra money and figured it would be easier if he didn't have to pay rent. But easier is not how he would describe his life now. *I guess when you aren't around something, you forget how bad it is, right up until you're back in it,* he thought.

Sure, things became worse between him and his mother when she discovered he stopped drinking noggy. He didn't have the guts to stop when he was living with her before, but as soon as he was gone, he purged that crap from his life. To say his mother became angry when she realized he wasn't drinking it anymore is an extreme understatement. She just kept repeating, "How dare you?"

As soon as he stopped drinking the noggy, things became worse but better at the same time. He felt those horrible waves of emotions sweeping him away more intensely, but he could also start to feel possibilities he hadn't before. It was the start of something more. What "more" meant wasn't clear to him yet, but he was going to find out.

He made his way out of the house and to his bike. He saw so many neighbors marching near lockstep—mothers and fathers wildly gesticulating with monotone children quickly and nervously making their way to the family cars. He shook his head, mounted his bike, and started pedaling to his school. He didn't quite see the point of going to classes. College seemed a waste of time, but that's what everyone did, so he bought into giving it a try. But, more recently, he felt he needed to break away. It was as if what others did would be exactly the opposite of what he would choose to do.

The scenery along the way was always the same: the crooked shapes of bodies in various stages of panic, anger, frustration, or, well, nothing. He never quite noticed the absurdity of those two categories projected onto people.

Two and only two options. he thought. *The Reactors react to everything around them, and the Insensors don't react to anything at all. I mean, look at them!*

His father came to mind. What a silly man to be like so many others he sees. There was an apprehension that stopped him from going further in those thoughts. Again, not a familiar one to him, not one he could name. It was as if he wanted better for his father, and maybe even better for…

Oh never mind. *They deserve no better, but maybe I do. Maybe there's more than the slop we're given to drink and these intense anxious feelings that seem to come in tsunami-sized waves as I just make my way through my day.*

Jeremy passed the center of town, finally nearing the school. He glanced toward the plaque prominently displayed over the courthouse entrance: "What has been will always be." The acceptance of this mantra seemed like a distant memory to him, but still close enough that the taste from saying those words made him wince. He was not the same. He could feel it, so if he wasn't the same, then what has always been might not always be.

When he arrived at school, Jeremy could feel the energy surge within him. He jumped off his bike, quickly locked it, and headed to class. He marched past Nick. Jeremy regards Nick as a friend, but now the word seemed hollow. It's because Jeremy feels the same around Nick as everyone else at the school—anxious and stressed, with all the stomach-gnawing feelings that Jeremy wishes would leave.

*If I want to get away from my mother, then why wouldn't I want to get away from Nick or anyone else here?*

The noise in the hallways was deafening. If only they had already became Insensors, it would be a hell of a lot quieter, and maybe I could think straight.

All the chaos around Jeremy evoked his anger and frustration. He felt the words, "shut up," form in the pit of his stomach and shoot from his mouth. The words echoed through the hall with no effect, except for a few returned volleys of, "You shut up!"

Alas, it takes years of weighted experiences to successfully become an Insensor—if one gets there at all. Although Jeremy wants more for himself than to be an Insensor, he sure would like the others here to get there faster!

He remembered being told over and over how everyone is thrown into this life as a Reactor, that each person is born this way. It is the burden that each community member carries every day of their lives. This burden builds the identity of each person. The burden is welcomed. Each person must bear the weight of their existence.

*I get it! I get why Mom is mad, If we don't carry the rocks, then who will?*

Then he glanced at his bag. *Am I being selfish?*

Jeremy cringed from that last thought. Where in the world did that question come from? As he stumbled into the classroom, he fought to recover from his flood of emotions while rushing to his chair before his knees stopped him. He quickly looked around to see if anyone noticed, desperately hoping the answer was, "No one."

Who was he kidding? Did anyone actually notice anyone else? As often as he thought all eyes were on his missteps, he noticed more and more that the only thoughts others had were of themselves.

Jeremy's embarrassment was interrupted by a stern call to attention. Mr. Citino, his teacher, was one of the elites as all the teachers were here. Not quite a Reactor but not quite an Insensor. Mr. Citino's half-hearted effort to teach the basics to the class was barely audible to Jeremy, especially after chanting the morning mantra that included those suspect words, "What was will always be."

Class couldn't end fast enough. Jeremy thought that Mr. Citino might be one of the few people he could dare ask a question to. Questions weren't the most popular mode of expression around this community—not that expression, in general, was overly popular. It was preached that questions led to answers, which led to rebellion, which threatened their way of life.

Jeremy thought about the questions he asked,

how they were answered, and the taste of the noggy. *Did my feelings start when I stopped drinking that crap? There I go again, asking more questions. There must be something to this.*

Jeremy's chance came when the bell rang, signaling the end of class. He began to walk toward Mr. Citino's desk, but his anxiety returned, driving him to turn away. He clenched his fists in defiance and tried to approach Mr. Citino again. Once again, his anxiety turned him away. He called on his anger to overthrow the power of his anxiety. He wanted desperately to ask Mr. Citino what was going on within him. He turned again, but stopped for a third time. Before he could make another retreat, he heard Mr. Citino's voice.

"Well, what is it, Jeremy?" Mr. Citino asked, looking down at some papers on his desk. "Are you going to walk back and forth all day? What do you want?"

Jeremy's eyes widened, and he paused before saying, "I've been feeling some new feelings and having thoughts about things that I don't understand."

"So, knock it off!" Mr. Citino snapped, still not raising his head or even an eyebrow of acknowledgment.

"Well, I'm not choosing it. It's just happening. See, I had this moment that I wanted something better for my Dad, and then I had this feeling like maybe I could be better than others, and..."

Jeremy sighed heavily through the exasperated look on his face.

"What do you want me to do about it, Jeremy?"

Jeremy could feel Mr. Citino's judging eyes on

him, making him want to run away for good this time. He could already feel the regret creeping in as his future memory from these moments was already setting in.

"I just wanted to know more about it."

The flush of red over Jeremy's face and the pit in his stomach grew deeper.

"That's not for us," Mr. Citino said. "That's for Them."

"Who are 'Them'?"

"They are Them. They live like that, but They don't tell us anything about that sort of thing"

Jeremy could feel his frustration building as his pulse thumped through his neck.

"Who are 'They'?" he asked.

"You ask questions, Mr. Citino replied. "Why the hell are you asking questions? Do yourself a favor and quit. Questions beg answers, and what was will always be, so there's no sense in asking. They don't tell us for a reason. It's better this way."

"Well, I want to know who They are." Where do I find out about Them?"

"God, you really are an obnoxious human, aren't you? There's a book."

"What book, where?"

"Where do they keep the books, Jeremy?"

"The library."

"Wow, you're a genius!"

Sensing this was about the extent of the information he could gather from Mr. Citino, Jeremy left the class with a mission. At least he had a thread to pull on, and pull on it he would. He rushed straight to the library, but when he arrived, he realized that he didn't know which book Mr. Citino was referring to.

As he scanned aimlessly around the library, his anxiety flooded his mind.

*What the hell did he mean by 'That's not for us. That's for Them?'* he thought.

Jeremy's eyes landed on the only person he could ask, but he already knew what her response would be. Ms. Goldston was an odd woman. She stood crooked with her bag well lined with rocks from the number of years she had to accumulate them. Jeremy tentatively approached her, trying to find the words that would match the desperation welling up inside of him.

"Ms. Goldston, Mr. Citino told me there's a book—"

"Oh, he did, did he? Well, there's a lot of books, so you're gonna have to narrow that down a bit."

"Well, yeah, I know there's a lot of books, but I want the one about Them. I want to know what They don't tell us."

Her head snapped up, and she glared at Jeremy so hard that he thought she was staring through him. "Never mind that, boy. That's not for us. What They do is for Them, and what They know is best left alone"

"Just tell me where the book is, and I'll decide what to do with what They know."

"You're an insistent little thing, aren't you?"

*Little thing,* Jeremy thought. *I'm bigger than she is and probably a hell of a lot smarter. What does she know besides where the books sit on the shelves?*

"God, you kids," Ms. Goldston grumbled. "Every once in a while, one of you come along. So ridiculous. Don't you know what was will always be? You might as well give up now. Everyone does in short order."

Jeremy was shocked. "There have been others asking these questions?"

"Oh, you thought you were so special. How cute."

"Where's the damn book?" Jeremy shouted.

She pointed to a room in the corner of the library and returned to what she was doing.

Jeremy rushed to the door and turned the knob. It wouldn't budge.

"It's locked!" he shouted again.

"Wow, how observant of you."

She opened a drawer. He heard a set of keys rattle as she pulled it out of the drawer and tossed it to him. As soon as he caught the keys, he spun around to face the door, then hesitated when he noticed a sign there for the mythology section.

This can't be right, he thought. *I'm looking for answers, and she's sending me to the mythology section?*

His frustration grew as he fumbled with the keys. The words, There were others, played a loop in the back of his mind, but he quickly replaced them with, But they weren't me. Finally, he found a key that released the lock and flung the door open to a dimly lit room. After his eyes adjusted to the light, he saw a large book on a pedestal

*That must be it,* he thought. *It's the obvious choice.*

His hands trembled as he grasped the cover and flipped the book open. A blank white page stared back at him. Undeterred, he flipped to the next page and the next, only to find more blank white pages in their lackluster glory. The tension within him climbed toward his throat as if what was within him was catapulting its way out.

Jeremy frantically flipped page after page to

see....wait! Suddenly he saw a phrase, "be compassionate." His stare penetrated the page as if the meaning would reveal itself, but nothing appeared in front of him or within him. Powering forward, he felt there must be something he can grasp, maybe another thread he can pull to find an answer, but every discovery was as opaque as the first. Fragments of thoughts, phrases unknown to him appeared one after another.

"He was kind," one phrase read.

"The journey was long, but it's within," another read.

"Find Purposeful Meaning," read another.

He continued flipping the pages to the end of the book but still had no answers. Just as he felt hope slip away, he saw a final phrase, "They live an Optimal Life," with a beautiful drawing of a mountain.

*A mountain,* he thought. He felt the intense gnawing at his gut release—a sensation he wasn't familiar with. Maybe, just maybe, there's a mountain. Maybe, just maybe if he can find this mountain, he can find Them. If he can find Them, he can find out what They don't tell the rest of us.

*I could be the one that finds these answers!* he thought.

He knew he was different. He knew he felt different. Now, he knows what he needs to know to break free of what he sees around him. As soon as the unfamiliar feeling came, it went, and the normal darkness returned. The feeling crept into his stomach and started climbing to its familiar resting place in his throat. *Where's the mountain? How am I going to get there? How do I even leave this place?* he thought. Doubt led to a feeling of despair, but momentary at most. His mother's voice echoed in his head, telling him how useless he is.

His anger emerged again to fight his anxiety, and fight it did! He slammed the book shut, twirled toward the door, and marched through it.

*No one can tell me who I am and how I am,* Jeremy thought. *I know what these people around me don't know and will find out what They know next!*

He ran past the librarian as she shook her head and chuckled. Her contempt fueled him forward. He skipped classes for the rest of the day. *What good are they anyway? What I need to know is not here but out there,* he thought as he worked his way toward the edge of his community.

The community's border wall came into sight but quickly left his mind—a problem he would solve later. First, he must rush home and get what he needs for his journey.

*Maybe I won't leave a note to scare the old lady into a tizzy,* he thought. Who was he kidding! Note or not, his mother would pay as much attention to his absence as she did to his presence.

The phrases played over and over in his mind during his ride home. But the one that remained the loudest was, *They live an Optimal Life.* He didn't know exactly what that meant, but if that's how They live, that's how he wanted to live.

After he arrived at home, Jeremy threw the basics into a bag and was about to head out the door when fear struck him so hard, it nearly knocked him back. He froze for a moment, which was long enough for all the thoughts trying to hold him back to rush in again: *Who am I to be doing this? I don't even know where I'm going. Who are They anyway? Who are they to tell anyone how to live? You know, it's getting late. Maybe I should wait until after lunch, just so I have something to eat first.*

Jeremy dropped his bag and looked around his room, desperately searching for something to distract himself from these thoughts surging through him. He sat on the edge of his bed, staring at the wall, hoping that it would tell him what to do from here. He reached for his bag again, but just as quickly, pulled his hand away. Finding something to do was never a problem until recently because what was done was what was always done: Get up, drink noggy, go to school, come home, drink more noggy, fight with his mother, go to bed, and get up to do it all over again.

*Well, I guess I could try and find a way through the wall that surrounds us,* Jeremy thought, shaking his head and still looking around the room for something, anything to do. He thought of how his mother kept labeling him a failure just because he left home, struggled, and had to return home to live with them again.

What's the point of anyone who's labeled a failure for life trying anything if it doesn't work out? What if he failed here? What if he couldn't find a way out? He thought of the snide comments from Mr. Citino and Ms. Goldston. He also thought of Ms. Goldston's comment, "There were others. If others had, why not him? He felt frustration, combined with another sensation less familiar to him, surge inside of him. It was just enough to complete the reach for his bag and move his body out of his bedroom and outside the house. It struck him how much easier his later steps were than the initial ones.

Without a plan and no more forethought, he headed toward the edge of his community. As the border wall came into sight, he stopped in his tracks. People just walk by this wall as if it weren't there. No one even looks at it. No one even notices that they are held into place by what seems to be an impenetrable barrier. The moment's pause seemed to usher his anxiety back, followed by a hopeless feeling. He closed his eyes to find an inner strength that would propel him forward and was nearly overwhelmed by the surge of thoughts and emotions. The overwhelming experience forced him to open his eyes to a different perspective of the wall in front of him.

*Hmmm, that wall isn't as high as I thought!*

Jeremy looked around, wondering if anyone ever noticed that the wall wasn't nearly as tall as it was believed to be. The feeling he felt after reading the book returned and began empowering him.

*I think I can get over that wall,* he thought.

That feeling grew and empowered him. He looked to his left, along the length of the wall, and saw something he had never seen before. It was an opening in the wall, as plain as day. He rushed toward it as if it might disappear if he didn't arrive there in time. It was indeed an opening, and it was not leaving.

Jeremy looked around to see if anyone else noticed the opening, but it didn't seem like they did. He decided to ask some people nearby to make sure.

"Do you see this?" he yelled at someone, who immediately ignored him.

He stopped a man and asked, "Do you see that doorway?"

"Are you a fool, boy?" the man shot back, then pushed by Jeremy.

"But it's right there," Jeremy said as the man walked away.

Jeremy pointed it out to another person, who

promptly dismissed him with a laugh.

Jeremy was about to say, "what's wrong with these people," but he already knew the answer to that question, the very question he was seeking to solve for himself. No one but Jeremy can see that opening in the wall.

He stepped closer to the opening to peer through it, but it was too blurry to make out what awaited him on the other side. He tentatively reached toward the opaque image, but the opening changed to brick. He quickly pulled his hand away as if the brick slapped him. Then the opening reappeared. He felt his weight push ever so slightly away, which forced him to step back against his will. Regaining his composure, he moved his foot forward to reclaim his position and tentatively reached out. Once again, the opening closed before him, denying his reach.

The flood of stress hit Jeremy like a tsunami. It overtook his fleeting confidence, forcing first one, then two steps back. He called upon his anger to overtake his anxiety once again, feeling sure that would break the opening wide enough for him to burst through, but...nothing. The wall was as solid as it appeared to everyone else.

He paused while he thought about a solution. What about that unexplored feeling that he has felt twice? What was it? How did it show up before? Ah, yes, it was when he thought about the possibilities ahead! So, he did exactly that. He imagined what it would be like to leave this community and find Them. He imagined finding the mountain. He imagined the reality of those possibilities, just for a moment, but it was a moment long enough. He wanted more. He felt he could do more, be more, achieve more. His feet moved    forward,    through    the    clear    opening.

# MISTAKES, FAILURES, AND TAKING ACTION

After taking a deep breath and widening his eyes, Jeremy turned his head from left to right to find any reason to retreat the way he came. He found none. In fact, there was a quietness, a peacefulness engulfing him that was as unfamiliar as the emotion that pushed him to this point. It was as if the typical emotions that were ever-present within him were out of place here.

He looked around. The colors were vibrant. The air was light and fragrant. He then thought to turn around to see at what he had just left. The dreary landscape, the only place he had known for his entire life, looked drearier than ever. Those people he left behind were still bustling along, unaware his triumphant passage. He wanted to yell, "How could you not notice? Look what I've accomplished," but he knew they would not respond. He knew better than to expect anything from those he abandoned.

Jeremy turned his mind toward his newfound direction. Pride swelled within him. He would find out what They don't tell them. He would find Them and find out how They live so he could live like Them. He smiled while he imagined his triumphant return and showing his mother and everyone else how amazing he had become. He ran, fearing that if he didn't keep moving, he would be sucked back through the opening through which he had escaped, as if his will to retreat would override his will to stay. As he continued rushing forward, he looked back every few steps until the passageway and the wall faded from view.

Then he stopped, panting from his movement and emotions. He looked back once again and realized that what was is no longer within the reach of his vision. As soon as those thoughts presented themselves, other thoughts flooded in.

"Where the hell am I supposed to go?" he asked.

Those words carried back the anxiety he hoped he'd left on the other side of the wall. His eyes darted around the landscape, and he started to notice the life around him. Everything was different. He saw trees in fantastic colors with elaborate foliage and brilliant flowers. There were bushes teeming with life that he couldn't identify. In fact, life was all around him. Wondrous creatures bustled about, none of which he could identify, but all of them seemed peaceful and harmonious. He remained still, as unsure as he'd ever been in his life. His feet sunk into the ground, preventing him from retreating.

"I can't go back, but where is forward? I hate my doubt when it shows itself," he roared. He had come this far, but was this as far as he would go?

"If only I knew where to go I would go, but I don't, so maybe I should head back. God, I hate this! I hate it when I do this! I majorly screwed up here. Who the hell am I to leave? Is it really true that what was will always be? What should I do? If only I knew more. If only I was better than I am. If only…"

He thought about that label his mother gave to

him—a failure, someone that could never live away from home. Is that true?

A voice tugged Jeremy from his thoughts.

"Why, hello there, young man!"

Jeremy pulled his feet out of the soft earth and tried to move away from the sound, but it moved closer.

"Oh, don't be frightened," the voice said. "You seem to be lost, and I wanted to see if I could be of help."

Jeremy's eyes centered on a tall, thin woman dressed in colorful, elaborate clothing that he had never seen anyone wear. There was a softness in her eyes and a gentleness to her smile that drew him physically backward but mindfully forward.

"I'm not scared!" he yelled at her. "I'm not scared of anything!"

"OK, my friend. I'm sorry to offend you. My name is Laluna, and my offer stands. Can I be of any help?"

The question was hard for Jeremy to answer. No one had ever offered to help him.

"Um, uh, um," he stammered for a moment, then managed to say, "I'm headed to find Them at the mountain."

"Oh, that sounds exciting! Do you know where the mountain is?" She looked at his clothes with what seemed like a familiar gaze.

*Who the hell is she to judge what I'm wearing?* Jeremy thought *Look at the absurd uniform she's wearing!*

"Well, yes, I mean, no not exactly, but it's a mountain!" Jeremy replied. "How hard could it be to find?"

"Well, it sounds like you feel sure of yourself,"

Laluna said. That's great! You seem well-equipped for your journey."

She motioned toward the backpack he had thrown together in haste and his bag of rocks that he instinctively held close. That's when Jeremy noticed that she didn't have a bag with her. How can that be? And she stood tall, straight even. At her age? How is that possible? He looked from his bag of rocks to her too many times to not be noticed.

"Do you have a question, my friend?" Laluna asked,

"No, I just need to get going." Jeremy looked around, unsure about which way "going" even meant. His anxiety returned.

"Well, I love an adventure. Do you mind if I come along with you? Meeting new people, what did you call them again? No matter, no matter. Meeting new people is always such a joy, and the mountains in these parts are a beautiful sight to see. I might be able to help you along your way."

"What? Help me on my journey? You're an old lady! What help could you possibly be to me in taking a journey?"

"You don't think older people can be of help?"

"Well, no! You'd just slow me down. I'm young and athletic and can make my way much faster without you."

"Yes, you certainly are in better physical shape than I am. I'm curious though: If you were to run a race against me, but you ran in all the directions except toward the finish line, and I knew the direct path toward it, would our physical differences matter?"

He paused. No one had ever challenged his mind

this way before.

"How about if you didn't even know where the finish line is?" Laluna continued. "How well would you fare in the race then?"

"That's ridiculous. I wouldn't run the race! Why even bother trying in that case?"

"Well, why indeed? Do you know where you are going?"

"Not exactly, I guess."

"Then you don't know the direction to take, correct?"

"No," Jeremy said as he felt his anger return.

"Well, maybe I have experience that can support you to take the steps forward that you need to. No one creates success on their own."

Jeremy didn't understand what Laluna was doing. Who was she to ridicule him like this, to make fun of him? But he kept going back to the fact that she walked upright. She didn't seem to be either a Reactor or an Insensor. Where the hell was her bag or rocks? How could she live her life without one? People carry the weight of their existence and bear it for all. Where was Laluna's weight? With all of these questions left unanswered and his recognition that the mountain in sight yet, he had to accept her company for now.

"Fine, if you want to tag along, then I'm not going to stop you," he said. He looked around, wondering which direction to point himself.

"That's nice of you." Laluna suggested a direction by pointing herself toward one. He quietly changed his steps to claim the newly discovered route as his own.

"You mentioned Them," Laluna said. "Can you tell me more about Them?"

*Oh no,* Jeremy thought. *She isn't stealing my idea so she can find out what They know before I do. I knew she was up to something!*

"It's nothing," Jeremy said. Just some people I need to meet with. It's not for you."

"What isn't for me?" Laluna asked.

"Just never mind. See, I knew you couldn't help me. You haven't shown me where the mountain is or anyone that can tell me where it is. This is a waste of my time. I'm not taking another step until I know where I'm going and how to get there." He folded his arms and planted his feet where he stood.

"I can certainly understand that. We watch forever pass by as we wait for it to begin. I wonder how close you'll get to the mountain without moving."

Jeremy stared at his feet as if they were at fault for his lack of progress.

"There's no point in trying to go somewhere when I don't know exactly how to get there," he said.

"What an interesting word—'try.'" Laluna said.

"What's so interesting about it?"

"Well, how do you try to do something? Don't you either do it or you don't do it?"

"No, because it might not work. You might fail so you try it, but you might fail to do it."

"And you think failure is bad?"

"Seriously? What a ridiculous question! Of course failure is bad! Who the hell wants to fail?"

"I do."

"Wha–, What?" That's ridiculous! Why would you want to fail?"

"Because I want to succeed."

"OK, I knew you were crazy, and you're proving

it. Failure and success are opposites. If you want to succeed, you can't also fail. If you know exactly where you're going and how to get there, then what you just said becomes pointless and meaningless."

"It sounds like you want certainty."

"Certainty? Well, yeah, I want to be certain about where I'm going and how to get there."

"How often have you found life to be certain?"

He looked back down at his feet, wondering if they would move him away from this inquisition.

"Don't you find life unpredictable? Don't you find there are very few things you actually control?" Laluna continued.

"No! I can control what happens around me and to me." Jeremy replied.

"You can? Do you feel that's the case now? Do you feel like you're controlling what's happening now?"

"Yes, I'm going this way." Jeremy pointed his nose in the direction his feet were already traveling. Then he paused and turned toward Laluna.

"Are you coming?" He was shocked by his actions and those words. But in defense of himself, he had never met someone like her or heard someone speak like she did. Maybe those thoughts and sensations that emerged when he stopped drinking the noggy have more meaning to him now. Maybe they were even behind the actions he just took. There must be something driving his current request.

After only a few steps, Jeremy looked to his left and noticed a large clearing just on the other side of bushes that nearly glowed blue. The faint call of curiosity grew loud enough to move him toward the clearing. With a smile, Laluna joined him, and

Jeremy's eyes fell upon quite a scene. It was a labyrinth, entirely within his view, with creatures of such variety that he had never seen throughout the pathways. The exit was as plain to him as his new companion right next to him. He was trying to make sense of what he was seeing: creatures of all kinds going in different directions with seemingly endless approaches to solving their shared dilemma.

"What the heck is happening here?" Jeremy asked.

"Well, what do you see at first glance?" Laluna asked.

"Um, I think they're trying to make their way to that exit over there." He pointed toward what looked like a clearly defined exit from the maze.

"Amazing what perspective can do for us."

Not sure what Laluna meant by that, Jeremy kept scanning the scene. He noticed some creatures that were toad-like, which moved on two legs. They had small ears, huge eyes, and enormous mouths that seemed to salivate from their movements. At every turn of the labyrinth that was clearly marked with a direction, they chose the opposite.

*What a bewildering thing to do,* Jeremy thought as he continued to observe. *What's the point of having a direction if you aren't going to take it?*

"I can't imagine they should be surprised they aren't achieving success in leaving the labyrinth if they deny learning from what they see." Laluna said.

"I guess not," Jeremy said. "What fools!"

"I can see why you would see it as foolish. I wonder how often we don't pay attention to the signs we're given in life that might help lead us toward something we want to achieve? It seems to me I've had to remind myself of that from time to time. Have you?"

"No! I listen! I wouldn't make such a dumb mistake."

"Interesting. You think mistakes are bad?"

"Well, of course they are. You shouldn't make mistakes."

"I wonder how you learn if you don't make them. Of course, learning is optional in those moments, but available if you're paying attention. I would love to get to my mistakes and encounter my momentary failures as fast as I can."

"Again with failures? I don't understand why you would want to encounter failure. If you encounter a failure, then you failed, and I'm not a failure."

Jeremy recalled his mother's label, his community's label of him. He failed to succeed on his own and had to return home. Once a failure, always a failure.

*Failure is permanent,* he thought. *Why would you want to fail in anything?*

As soon as that thought entered Jeremy's mind, Laluna replied, "Do you think failure is permanent or momentary?"

His pause gave her permission to continue.

"It seems to me that the faster you get to your momentary failures, but decide to learn, adapt, and improve through them, the faster you can achieve the success you are working toward."

Learn what? Adapt how? Improve what? Jeremy felt his embarrassment rear its ugly head, forcing him to turn his full attention back to the activity in the labyrinth.

He noticed wrinkled creatures that looked like

humans someone had shrunk. Similar to the apparently confused or defiant toad-like creatures, they had disproportionate mouths to their ears. They seemed to huddle and chatter incessantly, looking in every direction, including where to go, but going didn't seem to be anywhere near a next action. Just behind them, toward the start of the maze, faint-looking, nearly transparent creatures, stood perfectly still with only their eyes telling their story. They seemed to fade with each passing moment, with the fear on their faces being the only pronouncement they still existed.

"I haven't seen any of them actually move this entire time," Jeremy said. "Those seem to be stuck in their huddle." He pointed to the small groups in nearly constant chatter. "And those seem to be nearly disappearing while they just stand there."

"What do you think that's all about?" Laluna asked.

"They probably don't know which way to go, but there are signs everywhere. Why not just try a direction and see what happens?"

"You mean, take a step without worrying about making a mistake?"

The irony of his statement, highlighted by Laluna's response, stung him.

"Some would rather just talk about trying to do something, rather than actually doing something," Laluna continued. "It's interesting how the word, 'try,' seems to imply a lack of commitment and confidence, isn't it? Some may just be afraid. In fact, both cases are probably from fear, don't you think so?"

"Afraid of what?"

"Well, as you said, some people look at failure as permanent. If that's how you see it, then there's something to be afraid of, right?"

"I guess, but there are tons of signs and information along the way. They could just use that to tell them what to do."

"Sure, but what do you compare that information against?"

"What do you mean?"

"It seems to me they might not have a clear definition for what they want to achieve. I just wonder how you know what information to accept and what information to dismiss if you don't have a good start and end point, if you haven't defined what 'done' means."

Jeremy's gaze fell upon a tower just taller than the walls of the labyrinth. It had a well-lit and colorful sign that stated, "Start Here." So many passed right by the obvious landmark and started to scurry down random paths with momentary gazes at the suggestions laid out for them along their way. Jeremy began to feel something for these creatures. Was it frustration? Anger? What were they doing to themselves? While Jeremy pondered these questions, he noticed a new kind of creature. Their eyes and ears were much more pronounced than any other creature he had observed, but their mouths were disproportionately small. One after another, they made their way up and down the tower, pausing at the top to gaze into the distance and observe the exit. It was quite orderly, in fact. They diligently wrote on a small notepad and had brief conversations between them before heading back down to start their journey. Their long arms and fingers swayed slowly as they made their way equally slowly but steadily in the direction they originally observed. He noticed many such creatures from his omniscient perspective stopping at various junctures to consult the signs provided and their own writings. He saw some head away from the chosen path, but only momentarily. After consulting their writings and brief interactions with one another, they each successively reestablished their momentum with even more vigor than previously applied.

"See? There!" Jeremy motioned toward the creatures making tremendous progress on their quest. "Why not just do that?"

"Why, indeed?" Laluna replied.

"All you have to do is know where you're going, have it clearly in mind, pay attention to what people suggest, and learn as you go. What a simple game this is!"

"And ask good questions."

"Ask good questions? What do you mean?"

"Well, if someone was to make a suggestion or tell one of those creatures to change direction, they could ask themselves a question, 'Would that bring me closer or further away?'"

"Closer or further away from what?"

"From what they have claimed their success to be. Questions beg answers, so asking good questions of yourself can challenge you to think of an answer that would move you forward. How about for you?"

"For me?"

Jeremy fell quiet for a moment. He knew he needed to find the mountain, but the fact he didn't clearly define which mountain and where it could be a problem. He did accept Laluna as a companion, so that might be good. He refused to move, but now he is starting to feel energetic from within, which can propel him forward.

*Maybe it's OK to pick a direction and…what did she say? Um, learn, adapt, and improve through this. I can do that. Of course I can do that!*

He looked around again, and his eyes were delighted to see the tops of what appeared to be mountains in the distance. It was as if layers were peeled back from his eyes, which enabled him to see what was likely there moments before.

"There! There! That's where They are." He said this to convince himself. He looked at the ground in each direction as if he hoped arrows would appear. Then his eyes returned to Laluna, his traveling companion.

"Let's head to Nannila down this way," Laluna said. "I think you'll find it quite interesting."

# JUDGING OTHERS

They walked in silence for a time. Jeremy reflected on the labyrinth and all the creatures he saw. *You have to know where you're going in order to get where you're going.* Seems obvious, but clearly some of them didn't quite get how obvious that is. Like Laluna said, one must know where the finish line of a race is and actually move toward it if they ever want a chance of crossing it. And, of course, they have to get moving; otherwise, how do they ever make any progress? Another quite obvious concept, but overlooked by so many he saw. One can't just blindly listen to information and act on it, but they should listen and reflect on it. They should ask themselves questions like, "Will this bring me closer or farther away?"

The sensations Jeremy felt while lying in bed in recent weeks were more pronounced now. It wasn't his anxiety. It was...he wasn't quite sure yet, but it was warmer than he'd felt before. It was in proximity to what he felt as he discovered the exit from his previous prison. He didn't know exactly what all of this would mean to him, but he was moving forward and had the mountain in sight, so he was happy about that.

His introspection was disrupted by voices nearby. There was a small collection of shops with various characters coming in and out just ahead from where he and Laluna were walking. The characters were as similar as they were different, with very few having features consistent with Jeremy's. What a strange place this new land is turning out to be. They all seemed benign enough, but clearly more exuberant about life than he was accustomed to.

As Jeremy and Laluna continued their journey, getting a closer view of the scene, Jeremy noticed a short, pudgy man, carrying drink and food and walking with a companion on the way to the next store. Suddenly he tripped over a bulge on the ground, and his food and drink flew toward an unsuspecting passerby. Everyone who saw the man fall gasped over the calamity.

"Ha! What a klutz and a fool!" Jeremy shouted.

"Oh, you know him?" Laluna asked.

Jeremy whipped his head around with confusion drawn all over his face.

"No, of course not!"

"Oh, but you just said he was a klutz and a fool. How would you know that otherwise?"

"Um, just look at what he did and look at the scene he caused. Only a klutz and a fool would do that."

"You mean make a mistake and have a mishap? Surely you have tripped over something or made a mistake before, no?"

"Well, yeah, but I'm not him," Jeremy said as he looked back at the scene, chuckling.

"You're definitely correct there. You aren't him. Do you feel like you know more about him than this single moment offers?"

"Well, no, I guess not."

"We witness people in thin slices of their lives,

certainly not the full continuum. I wonder if you would feel misjudged if someone was to form the conclusion you made."

*Ugh! I wish I were already at the mountain so I could find out what They don't tell us and be done with this,* Jeremy thought. *Now I can't even call someone what they clearly are without getting ridiculed.*

Jeremy looked toward the mountain to reassure himself that it existed. It seemed fainter, almost out of focus, or at least not as clear as it appeared just moments ago. He began to panic.

Laluna sensed Jeremy's emotional wave by reading the expression on his face. She continued speaking with rushed words in hopes she could stop Jeremy's torrent.

"Do you think you'd ever really have all the information about anyone outside of yourself when you see or interact with them?"

"Well, no, how would I?"

"How would you indeed? Oh, judgments, condemnations, and general labels do always seem to be premature, don't they?"

"Because I don't know everything about them?"

"Exactly! It would seem to me, the longer I can wait to form those conclusions, the better it will be for both me and them. That's at least what I've found."

Jeremy paused, looking back at the scene as people aided the poor soul in regaining his original stance. Some offered their food and drink to the man, and others trying to clean the mess from his clothes. He looked down while he observed a new sensation that had become part of him. It echoed his feelings for his father, an expressed kindness as if hoping something would be better for another with an opposing feeling or inner regret at his initial reaction. The internal battle continued as he raised his head toward the faded mountain view, only to see it a bit clearer now. He smiled faintly as the scene of the fallen man in the village faded, and they continued their journey toward Nannila.

## MEETING YOURSELF

So many memories and thoughts flooded Jeremy's mind as they traveled toward Nannila in silence: *Judging others is instinctual, right? But it does seem unfair to conclude something about another with such limited information. But, what if you DO have information? Even still, you don't know everything about them, right?*

While examining these thoughts, Jeremy noticed his old lens was being replaced with a new one, which provided new insights from his memories. Reactors react. He was consistently judged and condemned by people around him in his community, his mother, his teachers—pretty much everyone he came in contact with. *I guess that doesn't make it right, but if it is instinct, then how do you change it?*

Jeremy also recalled the strange creatures he saw in the labyrinth and the conversations he had so far with Laluna. *Do others talk like her here?* he wondered. *Does everyone think like her?*

Then he realized that no one he saw in the village where the man fell had a bag of rocks. No one he had seen since he crossed the opening in the wall walked with a slant or a hunch in their backs. What made everyone so different here? He looked around at the beauty that the landscape held. His community was so drab, so lifeless. He felt peace here—a sensation he was unfamiliar with.

The silence around Jeremy and Laluna was broken by clamoring just ahead. A village with a humble entrance but a grand feel came into sight. As they entered, the full scale of the village came into focus. The streets were alive with activity. Laluna's pace didn't change, but Jeremy's slowed after they entered and approached a small crowd that had formed around what appeared to be a newly-erected monument. Then Jeremy stopped, well short of their goal. Laluna noticed and turned toward him.

"Is something wrong?" she asked.

"I don't like crowds," Jeremy said.

"You don't like when people are together?"

"Well, yeah, I don't like when there's a lot of people together and I have to be around them. My anxiety comes out when that happens."

"You experience anxiety when you're around a lot of people?"

Slightly confused by Laluna rephrasing his comments, Jeremy looked around for any distractions that could pull his mind away from the anxiety taking over his body. There were countless characters among the villagers, all different shapes, sizes, and expressions. Some were so extraordinary Jeremy couldn't help but take notice. As his attention widened, a flash of light, repeating itself several times, caught his periphery and pulled his focus toward it. The light was coming from a building, set apart from the others, just a short distance from where they stood.

"Oh, I bet the laimenters are discovering themselves," Laluna said, directing her attention to the building.

Jeremy, glanced at Laluna, then walked to the

building to investigate. Without wanting to appear too obvious, he attempted a casual walk by the window where the light was coming from. Unfortunately, discretion was not an option when his eyes found the source. He saw people packed in the room, but these were no ordinary people. The atmosphere in the room was chaotic as the people walked around, without any apparent purpose or direction. Some looked quite ordinary, but others were literally glowing, which accounted for the light that caught Jeremy's attention. Others had a sickly darkness about them. They crept around the room, with darting glances expressing ill intent.

One of the less remarkable people in the room nearly bumped into a glowing individual. Shock covered the aimless character's face at the same time Jeremy was taken aback by his discovery: The person who bumped into the glowing character had a striking resemblance to each other! In fact, both people appeared to be the same individual, except one glowed and the other didn't.

When the ordinary character stepped back for a moment of contemplation, Jeremy's eyes scanned the room and discovered another person—a creeping character that also bore an incredible resemblance to the original character. As this creeping character approached the other two, the ordinary character had a surprised look on his face as the trio met in the center of the room.

Jeremy's head shot back and forth between his new discoveries. His attempts at making sense of what he was witnessing were failing.

"So many are quite sure they know themselves through and through, don't they?" Laluna asked.

"What a surprise when introduced to both the light and the dark within."

"But they aren't within," Jeremy said. They are literally outside of him!"

"We certainly do project what's within to the world around us without even being aware of who we are and how we are, or even that we are doing it."

Jeremy turned his attention to the trio at the center of the room again, but noticed several others in the same situation. It was as if each person was being introduced to some version of themselves, one with a wonderful glowing light and another with a sinister darkness about them. He noticed that the light and dark versions of these characters started to move toward several people to which they seemed akin. The light tried to overtake the dark and the dark tried to overcome the light. Frightened by the potential outcome, several characters turned and made a dash for one of the doors. The light and dark people stopped the escapes by slamming into the retreaters' backs. The dark and the light were absorbed as a terrifying grimace encompassed the characters' faces. They were all thrown forward and almost lost their balance. Each person paused, flexed their arms, opened and closed their fists, and stared at their limbs as they moved as if they were reacquainting themselves with their bodies. Then they marched out the door with Jeremy's eyes following them with an intense gaze of anticipation.

"We get glimpses of our true selves, but so often, too often, too many are not prepared for the conflict and turn from it without resolve," Laluna said.

Jeremy watched as each person left the building and made their way into the community. He watched as one distracted a vendor selling their goods and pocketed what could he fit in his pocket before turning away with a smirk of triumph. Jeremy watched another rush into a casino to buy chips from the cashier. He watched yet another start confrontation after confrontation with each passerby.

"Such calamities they are, simply consequences of what they don't discover of themselves," Laluna said.

"What do they need to discover?" Jeremy asked.

"Who they truly are. It is harder than one thinks. Most are so confident they know themselves through and through, but there is no starting point to improve from if you don't know where the starting point is, truly is."

"Well, how do you know the starting point?"

"Taking the time to know the good, the bad, and the in between. It need not be extreme outcomes in all cases, but surely limits what one can achieve. This journey of discovery, my friend, is one so many don't take."

"Why don't they?" Jeremy asked.

"The habits that drive our lives. The cycles, the patterns that have us show up as we do. It is what we're accustomed to. The fear of the chaos that would ensue. But the chaos of change proceeds the triumphs of mind. It is the inner work, the inner journey that creates the opportunities. But it isn't an easy journey, especially when someone doesn't have the will to take it."

Jeremy thought about the journey he was on. At least he got started, right? Sure, he paused earlier, but he took his steps forward, not like those fools in the labyrinth that had no idea where they were going, didn't pay attention to the obvious signs around them, or didn't even start! Once he found Them and They told him what They won't tell others, then he'll know what to do. He'll find out what this Optimal Life thing is. Why does it matter who he truly is inside if he can just become like Them and live how They live?

"Once I find Them and They tell me what They don't tell others, I'll know what I need to know, so none of this will matter," Jeremy said.

"Why do you want to find Them and find out what They don't tell others?" Laluna asked.

"Because I want to be like Them."

"Well, who are you now?"

"What a silly question. I'm Jeremy."

"That's your name, but can't be who you are. Who are you truly inside?"

"Why does that matter? I don't see how it matters."

"It would just seem like not having a standard by which to compare the lessons against would make it hard to know what to accept and what to reject. It is much like wanting to take a journey that you don't have a starting point for. It would seem the more you understand about yourself, the more you'd be ready to evolve what's within toward what you want."

Jeremy felt overwhelmed from Laluna's suggestions. He turned his attention to the window again to see the same actions happening with different trios, except one person was curious as his light and dark partners approached him. He stepped toward the light as if to embrace it, first shaking its hand as if he said, "Hello," and then embracing the light in acceptance. The light absorbed into him, bringing a smile to his face. He then turned to the dark with the same series of embraces. The dark became slightly lighter with a lighter expression before it was absorbed . The character took a deep breath, with eyes closed, and exhaled in satisfaction. He then turned to leave, but stumbled a bit, catching his balance by stretching his hands in front of him. He shook his head while trying to recall how to walk again. His second attempt was slightly improved but still slow. With effort, he regained his focus and left the building to join the community. With a huge smile on his face, he rushed over to a small group of people. They were clearly people he was excited to talk with, share with, and celebrate his triumph with, but when he arrived, they each looked at him with skeptical eyes. They looked at one another, themselves, and back at him. Some simply walked away. Some chastised him as if his change were the attack they were defending against. The man's smile quickly turned to pain, and he dropped his head as he entered a bar. He quietly sat down, motioned for a drink, and tried to console his sadness in every sip.

"Why were they so mean to him?" Jeremy asked. "He seemed so excited about what he had accomplished."

"Sure, he might have embraced his true self, but what we realize isn't always what others are prepared to receive," Laluna said. "Our change is ours alone, and others have found their patterns that include who you were, not who you've become. What could be positive is received as a threat or a release of chaos in their own lives. It is very difficult to change when everyone else expects everyone else to stay the same."

Again with this "true self" she's talking about! Jeremy didn't want to ask Laluna about it and sound stupid, but his curiosity brewed as he listened to the language she used. Maybe he could ask Them when he got to the mountain.

# MEETING WHAT'S WITHIN

They left the laimenters to their discoveries and walked back to where the monument was being erected. Jeremy still felt the apprehension born out of his anxiety. Was that part of this "true self" thing? Jeremy paused to imagine if there was light and dark within him. Coming from his community made it difficult to imagine there would be much light to speak of. Dark? Well, that would be easy to imagine.

*But why would I want to know the dark? Why not just the light?,* he wondered.

Jeremy widened his attention and saw something unusual. He looked at Laluna and back to the scene he was witnessing with clear questions on his face.

"Ah yes, atometes are quite interesting, aren't they?" Laluna asked. "Having those pneumons living inside of you certainly can pose quite the challenge."

These odd creatures were shorter than most around them, but nearly as wide as they were tall. What was remarkable was their transparent skin. Jeremy could literally see within them. He wasn't exactly sure what he saw inside them, but he surmised it was the pneumons Laluna mentioned. They seemed to live within the atometes, right at the center of them. The pneumons were of various shapes, colors, and sizes. Some were louder, quieter, active, less active, but all within the confines of their host's body.

Jeremy tried to make sense of this while he scanned the street, spotting several curious creatures that functioned as a host to another. He focused on one at a time to see if the sense might reveal itself. He fixed his eyes upon a dullard atomete looking at what appeared to be nothing at all. The pneumon within was a pale red color that quietly spoke to its host through a long tube that reached to the host's ear. The pneumon's words didn't seem to faze the atomete, who continued his course with no noticeable change. Agitated by the host's calmness, the pneumon spoke with an increasing insistence while its color turned a slightly brighter red, but the atomete didn't react. The pneumon became more agitated while its color grew fiery, and its mouth revealed its urgent attempts at getting the host's attention, with still no effect. Suddenly, the pneumon ignited flames inside the host, with its eyes bulging and arms flailing, and the connection to the host's ear carried a torrent of sound. The atomete immediately responded by shooting his arms out to the side, coming to a screeching halt, turning, and wildly running away from—nothing. Jeremy kept surveying the scene in confusion, hoping to find the cause of the dramatic change, but he didn't see anything that would trigger it.

*What strange behavior!* Jeremy thought.

He continued searching for answers, first within his own thoughts and then in his surroundings. He saw more atometes and pneumons that reminded him of the first one he watched. Some of the pneumons inside the atometes were quiet and became more agitated like the first pair he saw, while others progressed from nothing to shouting and flailing about. He noticed other pneumons were somewhere in between, going from nearly shouting to fully shouting and a frantic state that resulted in a similar reaction from their host. He noticed one atomete walking toward a darkened corner of a street with glaring eyes coming from beyond what could be seen. As the host approached, a menacing creature appeared from the shadows. The pneumon inside the host became as frantic as the others, and its intense ferocity evoked the desired reaction from the atomete, who retreated to safety.

"Interesting pairs aren't they?" Laluna asked while watching Jeremy observe the creatures.

"I've never seen anything like them before," Jeremy replied. Why are the pneumons getting so upset?"

"Well, if you were being ignored, wouldn't you make a fuss about it?"

"Yeah, I suppose, but what are they trying to tell the atometes? One got really close to something that didn't look so good. But others seemed to be reacting to nothing. Why don't they just listen to what's inside of them? Why don't they somehow communicate and figure out what makes sense to do?"

"Real threats are rare, aren't they? Most are just perceived from within, but we get swept away by the perception versus the reality. Quietly listening to the faint sounds that are always there, but too often ignored, can build awareness to respond and not simply react."

*Sure*, Jeremy thought. *But Reactors react. That's what we do. How do I listen to what I can't hear?*

With that last thought, Jeremy spotted another scene with more atometes. There were several that were highly active, very animated, kind of all over the place. Their state seemed to mirror the state of the pneumons within them. Jeremy tracked one of the atometes as a passerby bumped into it, clearly by accident. The host's pneumon became infuriated immediately, which made the host ferocious. Then, the same atomete encountered three people, who wanted to engage with it, and the pneumon immediately directed the atomete to turn away from the trio. From one experience to the next, the host matched the intensity of the pneumon and took direction from it.

Jeremy watched another atomete with similar bizarre behavior. It walked quite a distance but then suddenly turned away as soon as the pneumon protested. Then the atomete returned to its starting point, turned around, and started its journey again, except over a shorter distance. The pneumon protested again, turning the host away. The host retreated to the starting point again and repeated the walk for an even shorter distance.

"Does this make any sense to you at all?" Jeremy asked.

"What do you see when you watch this unfold?" Laluna asked.

"Ugh! Why can't you just tell me what the answer is!"

"You believe I have the answer that you want to hear?"

"What I want to hear? I just want to know why these bizarre atometes and pneumons are acting like they are. I don't know why you have to make everything so difficult." Jeremy raised his voice and flung his arms in the air. "You answer questions with questions. Just tell me!" He stormed away as if he'd find the answers elsewhere, but then paused, and turned back to Laluna, who stood there with a gentle, welcoming smile.

"It can be the momentary pauses that we grant ourselves that can unlock our true potential," Laluna said.

He didn't quite understand what she meant, but did feel a new ability that was unfamiliar to him and certainly didn't align with the definition of a Reactor.

As Jeremy approached his original position, he began watching the scene again and discovered one of the strangest examples yet: a atomete fighting with himself, or more accurately, what was within him. The atomete clearly had a destination in mind, made apparent by the longing glances toward it that he could spare between his entanglement. But progress seemed to continuously halt the atomete's progress as the pneumon within him became agitated. The host's first attempt at making progress was to reach inside himself and try to cover the pneumon's mouth. When that failed, the atomete attempted to hold the pneumon down. Still failing, the atomete tried to pull the pneumon out of himself with such a strain that Jeremy could almost feel it. The atomete repeated this effort over and over until he started to fade from his original path to the point where it wasn't clear whether he was on one any longer.

"This is all very sad in a way." Jeremy said.

"What do you mean by that, my friend?" Laluna asked.

"This atomete just seems to be battling so hard against the creature within him that he isn't moving forward or getting anywhere at all. It seemed to have a direction it wanted to go, but it is nowhere near heading toward it now."

"It is difficult to live your life if you are beholden to what's within you. It is more difficult still to make progress toward something greater if you get swept away by the turbulence within. And the more you do so, the more beholden you are to simply react to what's within you and be less intentional with how you respond and move forward."

"It just seems like if you have to have one of those things inside of you, you'd figure out how to live with it better," Jeremy said, as he spotted a bit of hope among the insanity he'd witnessed so far. It was another atomete, but the pneumon within was less differentiated than the others. Jeremy could barely tell the difference between the creature outside and the creature inside. There was a tube running from the pneumon to its host's ear just like the others, but in this case, there was a tube running from the host's mouth to the pneumon. They were communicating with each other. As the atomete moved forward, the pneumon started to become agitated. The atomete responded by looking within, saying a few words to the pneumon with a peaceful gaze, and the pneumon relaxed. Then the host walked toward the darkened corner with the fierce monster as the previous atomete did. The pneumon immediately became agitated, and the atomete changed direction and glanced at the pneumon as if to say, "Thank you." The symbiosis between them was truly remarkable.

"Why don't they just do what that one is doing?" Jeremy asked.

"Well, why indeed, my friend?" Laluna replied. "It can be hard, can't it, to find a balance between hearing what's coming from within and becoming beholden to it. Too often, we aren't even aware of what's happening within us. Notice the breath you take right now. How often do you take them in a day?"

"I have no idea. I guess a lot!"

"Certainly a lot, isn't it? How many do you deeply connect with and pay attention to?"

"Well, I guess I don't."

"Indeed! Feel the rhythm in your chest, always changing, always talking to us, but do we listen? I think not. Our bodies whisper to us, but are we listening? When we do, do we immediately heed the warning? What an ancient instinct, so remarkable when it's needed, but so limiting when it's not."

"But there was something there to be scared of."

"Sure, at times in our lives there is, but most of the time it is a warning about nothing. We imagine realities that never come. We live in the wreckage of our future denying ourselves the joy of our moments. Imagine just being curious about it. Imagine asking questions and seeking to understand."

"Well, I can tell you what's within me. My anger, my anxiety, my…"

"You mentioned that before as if you are beholden to what's within you."

"Of course I am. We are all born Reactors with what's within us. There's nothing you can do about it until, hopefully, you become an Insensor and it mostly gets better. Noggy helps make it tolerable."

Laluna looked back at the small crowd around the monument.

"My friend, you can't resolve what you deny yourself to feel," she said. "Maybe if you lean into, as you say, your anxiety, in this moment, it will learn that there's nothing to worry about. Maybe you can teach it that you're going to be OK."

"How do you know I will be?"

"How do you know you won't be? This is about perceived threats versus actual threats. What real danger is there?"

"Ridicule and judgement would be what happens."

"Judgment comes at times, but not nearly as much as one would think. Who are you thinking about right now?"

"I'm thinking about, 'What if they judge or ridicule me?'"

"Right, that's what you're thinking, but who are you thinking about?"

"Well, me, I guess."

"You, indeed. Who do you think they are thinking about, then?"

"Well, themselves, I guess."

"We too often think the world notices us because we notice ourselves. But others notice themselves and only how they relate to you. And these moments are transient at most, momentary, a mere blip, don't you think? But much more important than the possible perception of another is the opportunity to teach what's within that you can do hard things, that you can lean into these moments. Resilience is a muscle built through resistance."

Jeremy thought how often he was worried about the judgment of others when there was no judgment present. And if he could see it, it was his imagined reality at best. The time he stumbled into this class just earlier today was one such example. He thought back to approaching Mr. Citino's desk, wanting to ask him a question. He thought about how his anxiety kept turning him away. Was he like the atometes he just saw?

Jeremy paused momentarily, joining Laluna's gaze at the crowd. He took a small step forward, a small step backward, then two forward, but then directed his movements back to the entrance.

"We really need to get going anyway," he said. "I really want to make some more progress before dark."

Realizing he hadn't quite planned where he was going to stay, his anxiety rose even higher. With arms flailing and panic in his voice, he cried, "I'm not going to make it to the mountain and back before nighttime. Where am I supposed to stay? I don't want to go back as a failure. What will they think of me? Oh, what am I doing? I can't believe I'm going to fail after all of this!"

"Is this your life, my friend, or someone else's?" Laluna asked. Her question snapped Jeremy from his momentary panic.

"What? What do you mean?" he asked.

"It is remarkable how we live our lives for others through worry and fear of judgment" she said. "When we do, we stop living our lives and we live theirs. It is best we live our lives as best we can and leave them to live their lives as best they can, then two complete lives can come together harmoniously. All of this is ahead of us, my friend. I know of a place ahead where you can stay, and you'll have plenty of time to get where you need to go. Let's start making our way there, OK?"

Laluna's words swept over him and released him

from the grip of his anxiety, and what was within quieted. He didn't understand everything she meant, but it still helped just to hear her words. He looked back at the atometes and their pneumons and reflected on the moments he just experienced. He recognized the surge from within drove his reactions. But he's a Reactor, right? Reactors react. But is he more? He wanted to be more. He has come this far. He left his community. That says a lot, right? That one atomete seemed to have such a connection to what was coming from within. Maybe Jeremy could, too.

*Maybe that's part of what They don't tell others—how to control what's within so we don't react as Reactors,* he thought.

# THE PATH LESS TRAVELED

Jeremy felt more propulsion than ever as they made their way down the path. He reflected on everything he saw in the village.

*I guess listening and paying attention to what's within is a good thing, but just reacting without questioning isn't a good thing,* he thought. *It seems like those atometes allowed what was within them to hold them back and dictate what actions they took or didn't take. But is that really how I've been?*

He instinctually pulled his bag of rocks closer and paused for a moment while feeling it. The bag seemed lighter. Fewer rocks were inside.

*Have I lost them?* he wondered while a sense of panic set in.

*But wait, I do feel a bit, I don't know, lighter, maybe?* He could feel his spine stretch and straighten just a bit. But just as he started to explore this new feeling, Jeremy and Laluna arrived at three diverging paths.

"Oh great! How are we supposed to know which way to go?" Jeremy asked Laluna. "Do you know which path to take?"

"Which way, you ask?" a booming voice said. "Well, it certainly matters to some but not to all."

Jeremy, startled, looked around to find the source of the new voice.

"Some choose paths at random, some with intention, and others still with aimless desire," the voice continued.

Jeremy's eyes finally found the source: a grand tree at the right of the paths had come to life to speak with him and Laluna.

"Um, I don't mean any offense, but I'm not about to start listening to a tree tell me what to do," Jeremy said

"Oh? Offense taken is my choice. But it's interesting that you don't find voices other than your own useful."

"I find my own to be the one that I can rely on. I guess sometimes someone might say something of use to me."

"Oh, how thoughtful of you. Arrogant learner it is, then, isn't it?"

"What? What does that mean? I'm not arrogant!"

"Whether you are or not is no matter, but how you learn or not is what's telling. So it goes. The naive learner thinks a single life form can teach them everything. As you are, the arrogant learner accepts no one can teach them a single thing. Then there is the truly wise learner that embraces a bit of something from everyone and all situations. Where do you say you are now, my lad?"

Jeremy looked at Laluna as if she'd asked this overgrown weed to dispense a lesson on his behalf. Would she really do this?

"Fine! Do you know which way to go?" Jeremy asked.

"Well, I know not what you seek," the tree replied.

"I'm trying to get to the mountain," Jeremy said as he looked at the mountain in the distance.

"Such a vague goal with such a hesitant

expression."

Jeremy sprung to attention as the tree slapped him with those words.

"Vague goal and what hesitation?" Jeremy asked.

"You are either going to the mountain or you are not," the tree replied. "If you try to go to the mountain, you will surely not."

"Fine! I am going to the mountain. Is that better?"

"Better, the same, or different is for you to find out, my young lad. But the mountain is a big piece of land to attend to. Care to be more specific?"

"You mentioned finding Them." Laluna said.

Jeremy shot a look toward her as if she betrayed him.

"It's no one's business but my own," Jeremy said.

"What an odd place to be," the tree said. "To be in need but refuse to be open to helping others help you. Fear drives you, my young lad, as fear drives many to either stand in place or propel themselves forward, for it is energy and nothing else. What you do with it is up to you. Sounds like you might be accepting the former and will stand where you are."

"What? I'm not afraid of anything. What I'm doing is for me, and no one is going to take that from me."

"Fear yet again, as if there isn't an enormity of bounty for all of us to share in. What you seek, my young lad, is knowledge. What you believe They will tell you. Am I right?"

The tree was too accurate and Jeremy was too anxious to get moving to deny what the tree said.

"Um, yeah, that's right."

"You are indeed in luck, then. All paths in front

of you lead to where you can be."

"Ugh! Why didn't you just say that!"

Jeremy looked at the three paths in front of him. They each seemed unremarkable. They were as straight as they were wide without an obstacle in sight. He shrugged his shoulders and started to walk toward the middle of the three.

"Interesting," the tree said.

Jeremy quickly turned his head toward the tree and said, "What is interesting, exactly?"

"Where you can be becomes so much greater through the perseverance of challenge," the tree replied while motioning to a fourth, unnoticed path. It was overgrown, and it had a sharp corner a short distance away, so it was it impossible to see what lay ahead.

"Listen, I just want to get where I'm going," Jeremy said. I want to get to the mountain, find Them, and find out what They don't tell us so I can know more than the others. Why wouldn't I just take the easiest path so I can get there faster and be done with this?"

"All paths lead you to where you can be, my young friend. It seems like your adventurous spirit led you away from where you were to here, as have others I've seen. It's interesting that you now set that aside to be so ordinary in your way, as others have been."

"Ordinary? What? I am not ordinary!"

"Ordinary follows the path of others. Extraordinary travels where few will go."

"But, but what about her?" Jeremy asked while motioning to Laluna. "I can do anything, but it might be too much for her."

"Oh, how kind of you, my friend, but I have traveled many paths less traveled, and I am here to do the same now," Laluna said.

Jeremy looked at all four paths, then looked down for a moment to contemplate the reality of his situation and hope for an answer to reveal itself.

"Maybe we should go back to Nannilla for a while," Jeremy said. "I don't think we explored all that's there. Maybe I can try and approach that crowd again. I really haven't eaten much, so maybe we should eat first as well."

"Procrastination and excuses are a plague, isn't it?" the tree asked. "Too much gets in our way. We await the cavalry to appear, not realizing we are the cavalry."

"What are you talking about? I'm just thinking of things we should do, or, well, could do before going, that's all."

"Ah, would, could, should, such limiting words. Let's will instead. Excuses or success, you can't claim both. Which will it be, my young lad?"

"I'm thinking. I just want to be sure, so if you'd be quiet for a single moment of my life, then I could think clearly and maybe I'd figure out what I should, I mean, will do! God!"

"Is that an anxious feeling coming up within you?"

Jeremy replied by looking at the tree with an expression that confirmed the answer to the tree's question.

"We know action is the only way forward, but then we pause, waiting for motivation to come sweeping in," the tree said. "We deny that action always precedes motivation. It is action, then motivation, then, guess what comes next, my young lad?"

Jeremy felt calmness set in, carried by his curiosity.

"No, what comes next?" Jeremy asked.

"Why, momentum follows, which only drives more action. Action shatters the binds of procrastination and gives to you the beauty of momentum, driving you toward where you can be."

Jeremy looked at the four paths again. He felt less weight from his bag of rocks. The lighter burden gave him an energy he hadn't felt in years. He let procrastination prevent him from leaving as soon as he could have. He let excuses get in his way from breaking free of the prison that was his community. It was only through action that he felt motivated to take the steps he has, and he could feel the momentum carry him through what he's faced so far.

He looked at Laluna and said everything that was inside him without saying a word. His fear coupled with excitement, and a sense of purpose started to well up within him. But he said nothing. She replied with a gentle smile and turned her attention toward the fourth path as if she knew he would choose it, and choose it he did.

# FINDING PEACE WITHIN

The first step on this path felt like one hundred were taken, not due to time, but because of the emotion Jeremy released. He remembered those same moments in his bed, those new sensations with new words and phrases revealing themselves during what seemed like a lifetime ago. But now, only a moment ago, yet another lifetime had passed by. He was standing straighter and taking fuller strides. He looked again toward his ultimate destination, and it was remarkably closer than expected! He started to see the details of what was an opaque mass, undifferentiated. Before he realized it, he had already turned the first blind corner of their new path. His action created intense motivation within him. He could feel the momentum set in with each successive decision to take the next step along his journey.

He thoughts returned to the labyrinth and all the creatures making various attempts, or none at all, to a successful exit. He wondered what excuses they were giving to themselves to not take action. It seemed so obvious now that excuses preclude success. Jeremy felt a prideful sensation that he listened to advice but also thought through it on his own.

He also thought about the atometes. That opaque place within him that evoked the negative sensations he struggled with seem to have so much in common with the pneumons. Was he simply a consequence of what came from what was within him? What was within him? Was that just a consequence of what he was around all his life? Was he really born as a Reactor? Was everyone else where he came from also really born a Reactor? The pneumons drove the atometes, but not all of them. Maybe Jeremy could achieve some kind of symbiosis with all the surges he felt within him.

*Wait, what did the tree say about others?* Jeremy thought. He had been so focused on the paths and his excitement that he didn't even acknowledge what the tree said about others traveling here. Was the tree referring to the others from Jeremy's community? How many others have been here? How far did they travel? What did they see?

"Um, Laluna, have you ever met anyone like me? I mean, anyone from where I'm from?" Jeremy asked.

"Perhaps there have been many," she replied. "Who can really say how many, but you are unique as you are the only you, isn't that so? I wouldn't concern yourself with others. Just imagine what you'll do, my friend."

As Jeremy thought about how to reply, a wave of intense buzzing sounds entered his ears.

"Oh look, fairies!" Laluna said with a smile.

"Fairies?" Jeremy shouted, trying to be heard over the incessant buzzing. These fairies were curious creatures. Small, no bigger than a finger, they darted about with speed that made their wings indistinguishable.

"I can't think straight," Jeremy said. "It's too noisy."

The fairies started buzzing around Jeremy's head,

which forced him to try to swat them. His hands waved aimlessly as the fairies avoided contact. One landed on his shoulder and smirked at him. Jeremy responded by shooing the creature away.

He looked around for the fastest path out of the chaos. As he scanned the scene, he saw a man sitting cross-legged in the center of the confusion. The man's eyes were closed, and his hands rested gently on his knees. The fairies were relentless, trying to break what appeared to be his stillness, but with no apparent results to show for their efforts. The man's breathing was pronounced but calm, rhythmical, in fact. Anyone could set a clock to it.

Jeremy continued to bat at the fairies, but he found that focusing on the man's breathing synchronized his breath with the man's cadence. There were moments where he could feel his breath more than the disturbance by the swarming fairies. But a tap on the back of his head from one of the harassing varmints broke the rhythm.

"I don't understand how he can just sit there, quietly, with all of this going on around him," Jeremy said.

Then he noticed Laluna smiling, celebrating the onslaught the fairies delivered. He shook his head as if the image would change, but it didn't.

"What are you doing?" Jeremy asked.

"Oh, my friend, aren't they wonderful?" Laluna replied.

"Wonderful? Um, no! They are miserable creatures—pests to say the least."

"What is within doesn't have to match what is around you. Inner calm and stillness is a choice to make."

Laluna continued smiling and playing with the fairies, who were now responding to her.

"Calm? Here? I can't be calm with all of this going on. Let's get out of here, and I'll show you how calm I can be."

"Being calm when everything is to your liking is no effort at all, is it? Choosing calm when nothing else is, well, that is the practice you can seek. It is mindfully intervening in the normal habitual reactions that empower the mindfulness we can enjoy in the moments we have, no matter what they are."

"Mindfulness? What does that even mean, *mindfully intervening*?"

"Finding stillness within to listen to what's coming from within. To let what's within come and go and be curious about it, but certainly not be swept away by it."

Jeremy didn't understand any of this. He looked back at the man in the center of the scene. The man rose slowly and gracefully from his sitting position and walked toward an adjacent path. His breathing remained the same, despite the fairies' increased insistence. The man paused, reached into his bag, pulled out a small piece of fruit, took a bite, and smiled in contentment. He continued walking. Jeremy watched the man until he was out of sight.

"There!" Jeremy shouted. "We can follow him out of this insanity."

Jeremy began walking quickly in the same direction the peaceful being went. Laluna followed, but she wasn't in a hurry. She was still enjoying playing with the fairies as she strolled along the path. When she finished, she caught up with Jeremy, who was now far away from the fairies.

"I'm so glad to be rid of them!" he said when Laluna arrived. "I don't understand how that being just sat there so calmly and you! You actually enjoyed them! How could you enjoy them like that? They're pests."

"It is interesting how we can have different relationships with what's within, isn't it?" Laluna replied. "It takes time and practice, but using what's within to find joy and contentment is what you saw, my friend."

Jeremy looked down and thought about Laluna's words. *I can have a different relationship with what's within?*

The images of his experience at Nannilla returned. But how? Is it even possible for him to sit calmly in the midst of such chaos? To actually enjoy the chaos?

*I'm a Reactor, right? That's not for me, right?*

The potential Jeremy felt was nothing like he felt before. The contrast between the man that sat in peace and found joy in eating a piece of fruit with chaos going on around him and how Jeremy felt was stark, to say the least.

Jeremy thought about the moment when he poured the noggy down the drain. How all the surging emotions within him quieted for a moment. What was that all about? How does one do that in situations other than those Jeremy was familiar with? The atomete Jeremy saw had a relationship with the pneumon that lived within him. That was the only atomete he saw that seemed at peace. But Reactors react, right?

Jeremy came here to be more. He came here to find out what They don't tell others. Maybe that's what They know how to do. That will be the first question he demands Them to answer!

# BEING SWEPT AWAY

Jeremy was happy at the progress they made. The mountains were getting closer. He wondered what his first encounter would be like with Them. What aren't They telling everyone? He couldn't wait to find out. He couldn't wait to return to his community and tell them everything he'd learned. He imagined his triumphant return. He would show his mother, father, and Nick that he knew more than them. He could show Mr. Citino and Ms. Goldston how wrong they were. He recalled Ms. Goldston saying that others attempted the journey but failed. He wondered why they failed. How far did they go? He still didn't know what those words meant, so how did they know if they never met Them? Maybe Ms. Goldston was wrong. Maybe she was trying to discourage him from leaving. He's thankful he didn't let her win!

Jeremy's attention returned to the path he was on with Laluna. They were approaching a bridge that straddled a river. Jeremy was shocked to see a new kind of being actually standing, or trying to stand, in the raging water. They were humanlike—tall and lanky with pale skin and obtuse features. They had big hands with long fingers, which extended their already long arms. Some had fishing poles, and others had nets. They were desperately trying to keep their footing in the rapids, but what were they trying to catch?

The thrashing water revealed the answer. Eel-like creatures rode the rough currents. Some of the eels were a pleasant yellow color with an almost angelic glow and hollow mouth. The others were a fiery red color, with huge mouths lined with sharp teeth. Jeremy tried to soak in this scene in stride, but it was hard to fathom. He looked at Laluna, his face pleading for an explanation.

"Well, these troggles are persistent, that's for sure," Laluna said.

*Troggles?* Jeremy thought. These troggles desperately tried to catch the yellow eel-like creatures, but often the fiery red creatures got tangled in their nets or grabbed their fishing lines, which threw some of the troggles off balance and sent them, screaming and flailing, into the current. . At times, the fiery red creatures attacked the troggles one at a time, hitting and biting at each victim until it succumbed and was swept away. Some troggles abandoned their nets and poles and tried to make it to the side of the river, to no avail. The fiery red creatures had their way with each one. Other troggles tried to hold onto their nets and poles and chase after the calm, beautiful, yellow creatures while working their way to the river's edge, but again, the fiery red creatures prevailed. One by one, the troggles were swept away.

Jeremy searched for a glimpse of hope in this chaotic scene. He noticed that some of the troggles had a peaceful determination. They held their nets and poles, but ignored the eel-like creatures passing by, even those trying to sweep them down the river. No matter how much the fiery red ones snarled and snapped at them, these troggles maintained an even breath and focused on the momentum they gained toward the river's edge. These troggles possessed a serenity that reminded Jeremy of the man who was not bothered by the fairies. This serenity repelled the fiery red creatures' attack. These troggles slowly, steadily made their way to the river's edge. Sometimes they struggled. The fiery red creatures temporarily threw them off balance, but the yellow creatures intervened, freeing these troggles from the watery fate the others suffered. Eventually, these troggles made their way to the river's edge and joined another group of troggles that Jeremy hadn't noticed until now.

The troggles standing on the shoreline looked into the water to watch the beautiful and dangerous creatures that passed by. Some troggles scooped the bright yellow creatures out of the water with their nets, held them and examined them, and then tucked them away in a sack. Sometimes a troggle cast a yellow creature back into the water. Other times, a troggle caught a fiery red creature, held it for a moment, shrugged its thin shoulders, and cast the creature back into the water as it snapped and snarled at the troggle with no effect. As soon as hope settled in with Jeremy, he noticed one of troggles grabbing a snarling fiery red creature from the water and holding it longer than the others. He stumbled forward, dipping his feet into the water. Another fiery red creature came and grabbed the troggle by the arm. Another one got caught in the troggle's net, weighing him down and pulling him into the water.

"Step back! You're getting too far into the water!" Jeremy yelled. "Throw them back into the water! You have to let them go!"

But it was too late. The onslaught was too much for the troggle, and it was swept down the river to join the fate of the others that were swept away.

Jeremy looked toward the river's headwaters to see where these creatures were coming from. What he saw was more shocking and completely confusing. There were troggles on both sides of the river, along with baby versions of the eel-like creatures. These youngsters had neutral coloring instead of the terrifying fiery red and the shiny yellow Jeremy saw earlier. On one side of the river, the troggles poured toxic garbage into the water, directly onto the creatures as they passed by, and the creatures absorbed the waste. On the other side of the river, the troggles poured a bright, shiny substance into the water that sparkled in the sunlight. The creatures swimming by absorbed this substance.

The outcome of these confusing acts were completely different. As each creature passed through the troggles' contribution to the river's flow, they transformed into the creatures Jeremy saw downstream. The troggles' actions at the headwaters affected the outcome downstream.

Jeremy couldn't believe what he saw. The troggles were the cause of the horror, but they were also the cause of the joy. Why would anyone allow those troggles to feed the toxic garbage to the creatures from one side of the river? Why didn't anyone stop the troggles dumping the bad substances and stick with the good? Wouldn't that make everyone's experiences along the river  positive and so much easier?

He looked at Laluna again, desperate for an explanation.

"Isn't it interesting that what you feed comes right back to you?" Laluna asked."

"I don't understand," Jeremy said. "The troggles could just stop feeding that garbage to those creatures and only give that glittery stuff to them, and all would be good and easy for them. Right?"

"Well, it is a choice, I'll give you that, but not an easy one. Sometimes one might not be aware of what one is dumping into their raging river and what the outcome will be. And others allow it to come from everywhere else, as if it is imposed on them, projected on them in a way. It is carried down the stream of their lives, sweeping them away from their hopes and dreams. And, yes, it is a choice but a difficult one indeed."

"It is their choice to let the bad ones pass by and only pay attention to the good ones, right?"

"Sure, but even those labels, good and bad, are values you are assigning to them as you witness them. Maybe they all are just creatures, equally the same, and only good and bad based on the actions and attention given."

"What? Clearly those red ones are bad, and the others are good. Look what they're doing to the troggles."

"Are you sure?" Laluna asked while she directed Jeremy's attention downriver.

Jeremy noticed that while the troggles were swept downstream, some broke free of the fiery red creatures, grabbed the creatures by the tails, and were led to a beautiful wading pool where the sunlight shined. Other troggles broke free and swam to the river's edge to join the troggles on the shore. The troggles directly in front of Jeremy grabbed at the fiery red creatures as much as the fiery red creatures grabbed at them.

"It is too often that we label good and bad when really, they are what they are and can be used for good or be our demise," Laluna said. "The meaning they have is the value we assign, nothing more and nothing less. All is our choice to make. But what we allow in will always come back to us."

"OK, but all those other troggles are victims of what they are doing up the river," Jeremy said. "Why are some still in the river fighting with those creatures and others are on the side of the river? Why do some get sucked back in?"

"It certainly takes practice to be able to get enough separation between you and all that rushes by so you can make your way out of the rush of it all. Otherwise, you are just surviving and not thriving. You certainly did admire our friend that found peace among the fairies, didn't you?"

"What does that have to do with this?"

"It is all just circumstances, my friend. We don't control what happens around us or to us, but we can choose how to respond. We can ask ourselves, 'Is this happening to us or for us? Are we victims or legends in our own lives?' Finding that peace within ourselves, without desperation, letting things go, just finding our breaths—all of it is what separates those that get swept away by what's within and around them and those that don't. Imagine mindfully intervening in those normal reactions and in what comes up from within to examine it, ask good questions about it, push back if necessary, and redirect toward the positive. Think of that singular example of the atomete: the symbiosis it found with what's within, to not get swept away by the bursts, but to mindfully respond in kind."

There's that idea again of "mindfully intervening." What is it? Mindfulness? It truly was incredible how that man wasn't bothered by those pesky fairies. He found peace in the chaos. Even his companion chose to have fun with the chaos and embrace it. And the symbiotic atomete was a unique example, compared to the other atometes who were beholden to their pneumons or battled with them. What did this ultimately mean, and how exactly did this relate to what he was seeing here?

Jeremy and Laluna finished crossing the bridge while Jeremy reflected on everything he saw along the river. It seemed like getting to the side of the raging river allowed the troggles to see what they wanted to catch and use and what they wanted to let go of. Gaining separation from the torrent and the onslaught of those creatures allowed for intervention.

*If you are in the way of the torrent of water, how can you enjoy the moment?* Jeremy wondered. *How can you see things for what they are? Is this what Laluna meant by mindfully intervening in what comes up from within? But I'm a Reactor. Reactors react, right? How do I mindfully intervene in what's coming from within? How do I get to the side of the torrent of thoughts that seem to persist, all the relentless emotions?*

"Surviving and not thriving," what an interesting statement. Those troggles in the river were barely holding on until they couldn't. Some saved themselves by letting go or even using the creature that originally swept them away. But, even still, there were dangers for the troggles that were on the river's edge. They seemed to get caught yet again by what was passing by instead of keeping their distance.

*I guess continued diligence is the only way to continue to be mindful of what's happening within you and around you,* Jeremy thought.

# WILL THIS BRING ME CLOSER

After Jeremy and Laluna crossed the bridge, they left the troggles to their struggles and triumphs. The mountain became clearer and closer. Jeremy was astonished by the progress they had made. It seemed as if their experiences from crossing the bridge propelled them forward, which accelerated their momentum.

The path led to a thick grove of ancient trees, which were quite beautiful. While admiring the trees, Jeremy wondered how many had passed through this grove during their lifetimes. He wondered if anyone who left his community were among them.

"Why, hello there fella," a raspy voice called out to Jeremy from behind a tree. "Where ya headed?"

Jeremy turned to see a small figure, thin and hunched over, with a long nose, sunken eyes, and coarse long black hair.

Laluna spoke before Jeremy could respond. "We are going this way, Straggert. He knows his direction well enough, but thank you anyway."

Jeremy hadn't heard this tone from Laluna before. There was a force behind her words that piqued his curiosity.

"Oh, come now, there's always time to chase the gold, isn't there?" Straggert replied.

"Chase the gold?" Jeremy asked.

"Sure, my young lad. Don't you want the gold?" Straggert asked.

"Well, sure, I'd like to have some gold," Jeremy said.

"Never you mind that fool's errand, Laluna said. "You know where you're going and what you want to achieve. Let's move forward."

"But he said there's gold, and you said I should be more open to listening and learning from others, so this is me doing that," Jeremy replied with a triumphant smile.

"Listening and learning from others is good, but the source is equally important to consider," Laluna replied.

"Oh, worry not, my fellow travelers," Straggert said. "I want what's good for you, and gold is always good. Am I wrong?"

Jeremy turned his full attention to Straggert and his back to the path he was traveling.

"What do I have to do to get this gold you speak of?" Jeremy asked.

"Oh, easy, easy stuff there, fella," Straggert said. "Just follow me, follow me, and you'll see. Easy, easy to get." Straggert turned toward an adjacent path.

Then Straggert handed a large bag to Jeremy and said, "First, I just need you to carry my bag, oh, just for a short bit, until we can get to where the gold is, just up a ways."

"Wow! This is heavy! What's in it?" Jeremy asked.

"Oh, this and that, from here and there. Nothing for you to see or care," Straggert replied.

"Why can't you carry it?" Jeremy asked.

"Oh, the burden of it," Straggert said. "I choose

to free myself of it when I can, but it's never far from my reach." Straggert pointed to the chain attached to the bag and a ring around his wrist.

*His burden? What about mine?* Jeremy thought while he looked at his own bag of rocks and his traveling bag. *But there's gold, so I guess it will be worth it.*

"My friend, we should really be getting back on our way," Laluna said.

"Yeah, yeah, we will," Jeremy replied. "Once I get the gold. He said it wasn't far."

"People are not what they appear to be at times," Laluna said. "Optimism is good, but with skepticism and caution is best."

"Oh, you worry too much," Jeremy said. "He's harmless."

"It is interesting how quickly we judge and conclude when we react to what we see and when it serves what we think we want," Laluna said. We ask questions of ourselves to serve what we want, rather than what we need. We seek to confirm, rather than seek to truly understand. We find only what will support what we've already decided."

Jeremy ignored Laluna's confusing concern and continued following Straggert. They continued down a path for a while with several twists and turns. Jeremy looked back to see how far he had strayed from the mountain. Now, it was out of focus. He could barely see the outline of the trees, and he felt his anxiety return. The weight of his bag of rocks, his travel bag, and Straggert's bag were harder to bear than Jeremy realized. He felt the weight bearing down on his back, bending him ever so slightly.

"Is the gold much farther?" Jeremy asked with a bit of desperation in his voice.

"Oh, not at all," Straggert said. "Come, come along now."

"I do think it is time to turn back, my friend," Laluna said.

"He said we are close," Jeremy said. "I'm not going to stop now! I want the gold!"

"What matters is not the treasures you possess, but the goals you've set," Laluna said. "Can you feel the momentum shift in a direction that may not serve you? Actions in the wrong direction will give you the wrong results."

"Oh, nothing to fear there, fella," Straggert said. "We are nearly there, you see. Ah yes, here we are!"

"Well, where's the gold?" Jeremy asked.

"Oh, gold, my naive soul," Straggert said. "The gold you seek you shall not find this way for sure, but alas, I have found relief for a short while to where I need to be, you see, so good riddance to you and yours."

Straggert stepped on a small pedal on the ground and the top of a stump opened. He jumped into the stump, and the chain followed him. The movement ripped the bag from Jeremy's arms, nearly knocking him to the ground. The bag and Straggert disappeared, and the opening in the stump closed behind Jeremy and Laluna.

Jeremy regained his footing and stood there, mouth agape, staring at the stump. He shook his head to erase his shock, pounded on the top of the stump, and stomped on the pedal. No response.

He looked at Laluna as a tear formed in his eye.

"What just happened?" he asked. "I don't understand."

"My friend, people are not always what they

appear," Laluna replied. "Yes, it is good to listen, to explore, to seek different paths and different opportunities, but there are questions you need to ask yourself when facing those turning points."

"Questions I have to ask?"

"Yes, for example, 'Will this bring me closer or further away?' is a great one to start with."

"Closer or further away from what?"

"Well, from what depends on the situation, but it is challenging yourself with those types of good questions that can ensure you are considering the consequences of your decisions. You are here for a reason, right?"

"Well, yeah I am, of course."

"OK, are you here for gold?"

"Um, no, but…"

"Right, and yes, gold is exciting, but that's not why you're here, and chasing it now doesn't bring you closer to your defined goal."

"Yeah, I guess that's true, but who doesn't want gold?"

"Here's another question. 'If that were true, then what?' It leads you to challenge the source of the information and how valid what you're considering really is. Why would someone offer gold as he did? If there were gold, would he just give it to you?"

"I'm not stupid, you know!"

"I think no such thing, my friend. It is a matter of experience gained and lessons learned. It is about being mindful of the emotions we experience that might drive us farther from our goals. Mindful intervention can come from these questions that challenge us. They inject reason to add to the emotion that, when combined, can be very powerful indeed.

One without the other is half of what propels you toward success."

"Will this bring me closer or further away from reaching the mountain and finding out what They don't tell others?"

"Exactly!"

"If that were true, then what? Why would someone randomly offer me gold?"

Right again, my friend. Finishing what you've started. Staying focused on the success you've defined. Taking inspired action toward your defined success creates motivation that empowers momentum, which propels you forward. Of course you want to learn, adapt, and improve along your way, but just as our friends in the labyrinth found, heading in every which way but toward your finish line will certainly not bring you closer to it. Shall we move forward positively and leave this as a lesson learned?"

"OK, I can do that."

Then Jeremy noticed that the mountain, although not back to its previous clarity, was less blurry. He sighed in relief and started the trek to regain that wonderful feeling of momentum he felt before his encounter with Straggert.

# WHAT WAS SIMPLY WAS

Jeremy and Laluna arrived at the spot where they encountered Straggert.

As a million thoughts about his experiences with Straggert swirled in Jeremy's head, he felt his anger and anxiety return. *Why did I listen to him? Why didn't I realize how stupid that was? Ugh! Why didn't I just keep going? I could have done this before now, anyway. Why didn't I leave that stupid place sooner?*

Then his thoughts returned to the pneumons. *Laluna said it was a choice. It didn't feel like a choice to not be driven by what's within! But is it? Could I choose to not feel this so strongly? Ugh! Maybe I've wasted all my time! Why didn't I just leave that place sooner?* Jeremy felt like his head was spinning on that last thought.

"Oh! We'd better go around," Laluna said. "Things can get a bit out of hand with those reggrats."

Jeremy snapped out of his spiral in time to see a chaotic scene. What Laluna called a reggrat was walking, or more accurately, trying to walk along the path. What looked like small lockers were appearing, opening up, shooting small books at the reggrats, closing, and then disappearing. Each book hit a reggrat, causing pain and distress and slowing their progress. The appearance and disappearance of the lockers had no predictable pattern. The onslaught was relentless and painful for Jeremy to watch.

Then Jeremy noticed another reggrat in a similar situation, but this time, whenever a locker appeared and launched its contents, the reggrat changed direction. As a result, the reggrat wandered in random directions and became confused on where it was really going.

Jeremy saw another reggrat dodging books, but this time, there seemed to be a finality to the experience. A single locker appeared, and the book flying through the open door hit the reggrat, returned to the locker, and repeated the cycle. After repeated attacks, the reggrat stopped and fell to its knees. It looked up and around as if it was seeking guidance or help from somewhere or someone, but no response came. The bombardment continued until the reggrat fell to the ground, covered its head, and curled into a ball. The pain on its face told the story as the relentless attack continued. The reggrat made several attempts to regain its strength and get up, but to no avail. When the reggrat stopped moving, the locker disappeared.

Jeremy wanted to step forward, to take some action, any action. *Who am I to do anything?* he thought. *There's nothing I can do. I'm on my own journey anyway. It's probably too late for the reggrat.*

He looked farther down the path and saw another reggrat, but a different scenario was unfolding. This reggrat had a companion that resembled a fairy, but it was slightly bigger and wasn't pestering anyone. Each time a locker appeared, the door remained shut. The reggrat and the fairy were talking, and in some cases, nearly arguing. There were times the locker simply disappeared. Other times, the fairy went to the locker with a key, opened it, removed the book, and delivered it to the reggrat. The reggrat briefly looked at it, handed it back to the fairy to be replaced in the locker, and then the locker disappeared.

This pattern continued several times. The reggrat had a clear destination in mind and was heading in that direction. When a locker appeared, it sometimes paid no attention and continued on its way. Other times, after the reggrat read the book the fairy retrieved from the locker, it slightly changed the direction to its destination. Something it read in the book caused it to adjust course. Sometimes when the reggrat read a book, it became distressed and quickly handed the book back to the fairy to return to the locker. The fairy was happy to oblige, but first, it scolded the reggrat in hopes of ensuring that this would be the last time the reggrat accepted that locker's content.

"I'm at a loss of words here." Jeremy said while looking at Laluna. He hoped she could provide some clarity.

"How often we allow what was to return, as if it would serve the needs of our moments," Laluna said. "How little we push back. How little we insist that what was remains where it belongs, under the protection of the protector within us. The emotional fortitude to stay looking forward and not behind."

Laluna's voice expressed a passion that Jeremy hadn't heard so far during their journey. Her tone helped him focus on her words.

"But that reggrat didn't have that problem," Jeremy said.

"It's amazing what you can do by challenging the desire to go back to what was," Laluna said. "Is it necessary? Does it serve your needs now? Is it empowering you forward? You cannot see where you are going and make your way forward if you are looking behind you all the time. Mindfully grounding ourselves in the moments we have will drive us forward to the life we deserve. What was..."

"...will always be!" Jeremy interrupted. "Right? What was will always be?"

"Oh, my friend! Certainly not! What was is just what was. What will be is within the power of your moment. What was can influence, but never dictate what will be. Too often, we welcome the past into our present when it has no business there. Dragging the baggage of what was can only limit our thinking, limit our possibilities."

"But doesn't the past teach us what we need to know? We can't forget about our past, right?"

"It isn't a matter of forgetting your past, but only entertaining the thoughts that serve us for our future success. You can learn from your past, influence your future, but direct your moment to the success you've defined. But define it you must. Our friends in the labyrinth found their way only when they knew what their success looked like."

"But all I know is what's come before me, so how do I know more than I've seen before?"

"Through action, my friend. Who you have been does not dictate who you can be. The past is the realized potential of infinite possibilities, but your future is the unrealized potential of infinite possibilities. Every decision we make that drives the actions we take creates our future that quickly becomes our past. See, we live on a razor-thin line between the past and the future. That is our moment!

Your thoughts are not who you are, but who you've been. Thoughts are just revealed memories. You don't create anything new from them because they are rooted in the past. The past is gone. It only lives in your mind. If you want to create something, anything new, you have to take action. And, if you want better thoughts, take inspired action to create inspired moments that inspire positive thoughts. It is all within you to take the action to create new memories that become the thoughts you reflect on."

"Inspired action? Is that what I did when I left my community?"

"That was certainly inspired action, my friend. Massive, inspired action. And the more you stay true to your course, the more you keep making decisions to move forward on your journey, the more inspired you will be. The patterns of our past can't withstand the force created when we love ourselves enough to leave the negative behind and move forward positively."

Jeremy fell silent. This was a lot for him to understand and accept. His community was built on the idea that "what was will always be" and "you carry the weight of your existence and bear it for all."

Laluna was saying that he could be more and do more. She was saying what was simply was, but what will be is up to him. It seemed like she was saying he could leave what was behind him, but how?

Jeremy glanced at his bag of rocks. Each rock represented the events of his life, the experiences he had and shared with others. They were imposed on him without any semblance of a choice he could recall. Did he have a choice now?

If thoughts are just revealed memories and all the

experiences Jeremy has had since arriving here have become new memories, then wouldn't his thoughts be more like those that lived here and not those of his community?

That thought inspired Jeremy to move forward. He wanted to leave behind his memories of the community. But was he ready?

*I need to get to the mountain first,* Jeremy thought. *They will tell me what I need to know so I can fully understand what she means.*

Infinite possibilities? Are there really infinite possibilities for him to achieve success? He wanted so much to find Them and find out what They don't tell everyone. Is that his ultimate success? Finding Them at the mountain? Is it possible there is even a greater success than that?

# WHAT WE CONTROL

Jeremy and Laluna had been walking for a long time. Jeremy had been so excited and focused on his journey and all the happenings around him that he forgot about eating! His stomach growled in protest.

"Oh, aren't you just famished?" Laluna asked, clearly having heard the call of Jeremy's hunger.

"We can stop in Fujala," Laluna said. "It's just ahead, my treat!"

Jeremy felt thankful, which was an odd feeling for him, but there was no other way to describe it. He had to accept that he would be lost on this journey without Laluna, his companion. Not only has she been his physical guide, helping him through the twists and turns, but she also emotionally and mentally helped him decipher these incredible experiences. He recalled the phrases he found in the book at the library: "Purposeful Meaning" and "Optimal Life." He still didn't understand what they meant, but he felt it was more possible than ever that he'd find out and it would make sense to him once he found Them.

They arrived at Fujala, a bustling town with all kinds of life. Some characters looked familiar to Jeremy, and some were new. They made their way to a restaurant just a few buildings down from the main entrance to the village. When they approached the door, Jeremy could hear the crowds from within. His stomach and Laluna's determined steps encouraged him to enter. But, once inside and the crowded space came into sight, he paused. He felt the familiar feeling of his anxiety return. He thought back to the crowd in the village earlier that day.

*What did Laluna say?* Jeremy thought. *I should 'lean into' the feelings to teach my anxiety that there's really nothing to worry about. I mean, what's really the big deal, right? I don't know anyone, and they don't know me. The more I act like a Reactor, the more I'll feel like a Reactor. That seems to be what she's saying to me. Besides, I'm hungry, so why should I let this anxious feeling that isn't even helping me stop me from finally eating?*

With newfound determination, he stepped forward, took the necessary steps past the diners, and found a chair on which to anchor himself. It was a triumph. Nothing bad happened. Nothing at all happened besides getting closer to being able to satiate his hunger. The anxious feeling abated, and he felt as if it might not return so readily next time.

Regarding his hunger and food, Jeremy had no idea what to expect. His guess was the food would be far removed from noggy and the bland offerings they called food in his community. A waiter came to the table and welcomed them with a huge smile and extended right hand.

"I'm so glad you've joined us, and it's so good to see you Laluna," the waiter said. "Shall I bring you the house favorites as usual, my friend?"

"Sure! That sounds perfect," Laluna said. "Jeremy here will certainly enjoy something that, I'm guessing, is out of the ordinary for him as most of his journey has been."

Jeremy thought about protesting, but his trust had grown in his companion. Look at how far he had come on his journey! He felt the shifts continue within him, and he was more open than ever to the experience what was to come. The idea that new action creates new memories, which creates new thoughts, repeated in his head. He wanted to experience more here to usher in these new thoughts. Besides, he was famished, so short of a creepy crawly of some kind, he was ready to eat whatever came his way.

"Sounds great!" the waiter said. "I'll be back shortly. I'm so glad to see another make it beyond what held them back before."

Whom was the waiter referring to? Was it others from Jeremy's community? Jeremy wanted to ask, but he was too hungry to think straight. Instead, he looked around to take in the variety of characters here, and there were plenty! He noticed some atometes with their characteristic pneumons inside of them, but these atometes were different. They were busy engaging in various conversations and interacting with others in the restaurant. What was taking place as the conversations continued was very odd indeed. The actual words from the mouths of those around a atomete went directly into its pneumon's mouth. The pneumon was literally being fed what the others said.

As Jeremy continued to watch, he noticed that it wasn't just the words of others, but also the words of the atomete itself that made their way to the pneumon. What came next would have completely shocked Jeremy before entering this new world, but he was ready to take what he witnessed more in stride than he ever thought possible. The pneumon inside each atomete emoted energy from its body into its hands. It formed the energy into a ball, and then, well, what came next surprised Jeremy, despite what he had seen so far. One of the pneumon shot the ball of energy through the atomete's mouth, hitting a poor soul in front of the atomete, which provoked a response of anger and frustration from the victim. Other times, the ball of energy shot throughout the body of the atomete, driving actions of anger and the appearance of fear. And other times, the energy drove positive responses from the atomete that others received with joy. There were so many variations that it was overwhelming for Jeremy, but what was clear was that the energy the pneumon created and used against its host was driving its host's reactions with clear and direct consequences to the atomete and those around it.

A particularly violent explosion immediately caught Jeremy's attention. The pneumon inside one atomete was emitting huge balls of red hot energy throughout the atomete's body with some of it escaping through the atomete's mouth, bombarding others around it. The crowd around the atomete didn't take this lightly and started to berate the atomete by yelling, screaming, and pointing their fingers in disgust. Every reaction that came from them fed into the pneumon. The more the pneumon was fed, the more its energy dissipated, and the pneumon gradually turned black. It cracked, split, and splintered inside the atomete.

Watching the scene gave Jeremy a sick feeling. The atomete started to fade, as if it were shrinking from existence. The barrage of hate and insults continued, and the downward trajectory followed.

The atomete tried to move away, but the crowd followed. The atomete's movements slowed as his appearance became less and less distinct from his surroundings. He reached out and pleaded for them to stop, but the crowd's berating continued. The pneumon began to crumble from the weight of what it received, until finally, it turned to ash, and the atomete vanished. The crowd returned to what they were doing as if nothing happened. But Jeremy couldn't resume anything. He stood there, paralyzed, terrified, and saddened by what he just witnessed.

He looked at Laluna with pleading eyes, hopeful for a consoling word. But she, too, was shaken, except she didn't have a surprised look on her face like Jeremy.

Jeremy finally broke the silence between them by asking, "Wh-what happened?"

"What we serve to what's within and what is served to what's within will be regurgitated right back to us and others," Laluna replied.

"I don't understand."

"We have to be very careful about what we allow around us and what we allow out of our minds and into this world because it comes right back into us. It becomes part of us, stored within us, and it is what we become. It becomes what we know. It becomes how we show up and respond to our lives. It can also lead us down a dark path of desperation and ultimately to oblivion."

"But that atomete seemed to respond in a nice way and got a nice response back."

"Sure, but was it intentional? Was it a choice mindfully made to serve its needs and those around it, or was it simply a consequence of what was given within?"

"So many of them seemed so angry."

"What you see isn't the emotion, but the choice to react to the emotion. See, we don't fear anger, we fear the actions associated with anger. We don't fear the emotions, we fear the actions associated with the emotions and the consequences of those actions. It is our choice to use the emotions or be swept away by the emotions."

"So, we should control our emotions, control our thoughts, and control how other people act toward us. We should make people treat us better, then we will receive positivity, and if we control our emotions and thoughts, then we will only have positive thoughts and emotions."

"I understand why you would suggest this, my friend. The challenge is you don't control any of what you just stated."

"What? Of course I do!"

"Let's work through this together. When you have attempted to control someone in your life, how did that seem to go for you and them?"

Jeremy paused and thought about his mother. The answer, he had to admit, was it didn't go well at all.

"Not well, I guess," he admitted.

"When you focused on controlling your circumstances and events around you, did you have much success?" Laluna asked.

"Um, I guess not."

"We control two and only two things in our lives: how we prepare to respond to our lives and how we actually respond to our lives. That's it! This is the inner work we all have to do. The more we focus on the externals, the more we miss the opportunity to change what really matters, what's within. If we focus on what's within, then no matter what happens around us or to us, we have prepared to respond, and we actually respond with intention and with purpose. We start to be effective in our lives and use our energy wisely toward success."

"But why not control the emotions and thoughts?"

"It is more about being willing to accept what comes from within. No need to suppress, oppress, or attempt control. That only grows what you are looking to change. Where you put your focus grows. Just be willing to accept it and let it pass on by."

"Like the troggles on the river?"

"Exactly! No need to be swept away by it all. Besides, we don't choose what comes up from within us. So much is done on our behalf, and what a glorious thing it is! The beautiful machine that is you runs so well without having to make a single choice, but there's a consequence to so much automation. We become a calamity in our own lives."

"A calamity?"

"Yes, simply reacting to the thoughts and emotions that are served to us instead of responding with intention based on what is given to us, put together with mindful intervention to use what's given to direct toward a greater existence. Imagine the wonderful questions we can ask ourselves."

"Like, if that were true, then what?"

"Yes! Exactly my friend! What is served up from within is just information and energy to be used for our purposes, to serve the needs of the moment. Nothing to run away from, suppress, oppress, or fear.

Notice the thoughts that arrive from within us. Do you choose them?"

"Sure, I choose my thoughts all the time."

"You do? Are you sure? How would that work exactly?"

Jeremy paused to allow Laluna to continue.

"If you could choose your thoughts, you'd have to have the thought before you had the thought. Choosing implies consciousness, conscious intervention. Thoughts just appear and are not the same as thinking. Thinking is what you do once you become aware of what arrives from within you."

"Yeah, I guess that's true."

"So, if what arrives is just what we serve ourselves, shouldn't we be mindful of what it is we serve ourselves?"

"Well, how do I do that?"

"It is all about the language we use, the stories we tell ourselves, our personal narratives."

"The language we use? The stories and our personal narratives? I'm not sure what you mean."

"If what comes back to us is what we serve to ourselves, wouldn't it make sense to feed ourselves only the good, positive, powerful, and empowering? The words we choose, the way we describe ourselves and our lives, it all comes back to us. What's within is always listening, ready and waiting to serve what we give to it right back to us. We then get swept away by the same."

Jeremy recalled the raging river. The troggles were responsible for feeding those creatures and turning them into what they were.  So, the troggles were victims of their own actions.

*What we serve to ourselves, it regurgitates right back to us,*

Jeremy thought as he looked behind him, where he saw an example that gave him the hope he was looking for.

Another atomete with a pneumon created a ball of energy and released it, but the atomete absorbed it, paused, pondered, and responded to the situation it was facing with joy. The pneumon made another attempt with the same response from the atomete. After a few iterations, the pneumon's release became symbiotic to the atomete's situation. It reminded Jeremy of the atomete he saw earlier. This atomete and the previous one shared an achievement. A symbiotic relationship was formed where what was served from within served the moment.

"Is that living with intention?" Jeremy asked. His question surprised him, as well as Laluna.

"You are so right indeed, my friend," she replied. "Preparing to respond and actually responding to your life with intention is an achievement that allows true success. Imagine the relationships that living that way empowers. Imagine the life one can live?"

The intensity of what he just witnessed needed time to process and settle in his mind. Satiating his hunger would be a great first step in making that happen. Thankfully, the waiter returned with their food.

"You know, my friend, there is so much we can learn about each other over a nice meal, don't you think?" Laluna asked.

"Like what?" Jeremy asked as he looked at the food placed in front of him. There was a plate with an incredible variety of fruits and vegetables. There was a bowl of soup for each of them with a fragrance that filled his nose with joy. There were breads and cheeses and cookies for dessert. Everything he saw was a far cry from the noggy and the bland, tasteless foods he was used to in his community. Excitement and hunger drove him to dive in.

"Well, are you ever curious about me, about others?" Laluna asked.

"No, not really. Everyone's the same. Well, I guess everyone where I'm from is the same. Besides, questions aren't exactly welcomed where I'm from," Jeremy replied while chewing a mouthful of the delicious food.

"Indeed, that seems clear, but questions here are certainly welcome and encouraged. Do you want to ask one and be asked one?"

"Um, I don't know. Maybe."

"Let's give it a go and see what happens. Here, I'll go first. What are you grateful for?"

"Grateful? What would I be grateful for?"

"Certainly plenty of things. The air in your lungs, the vision you have, the wonderful food you're eating, the conversation we're having, so many things to be grateful for."

"All of that is just normal. Everyone has those things. Why be grateful for it?"

"Not everyone is still with us drawing breath. Not all can see. Not everyone has money to buy food, and many are terribly alone."

Jeremy pondered Laluna's words while she continued.

"What a wonderful thing, gratitude. We can always take a moment each and every day to be grateful for something, anything. We can say it aloud, We can write it down. We can share it with others. What an impact that can have!"

"Um, OK, what are you grateful for then?"

"I'm grateful for having met you and for you allowing me to take this journey with you."

"OK, then, I think I'm grateful for the same. I mean, I'm grateful that we met and that you're helping me get to the mountain. I do think I'd be quite lost without the help."

"Thank you, my friend, and how did that make you feel, saying that?"

"Good in a way, I guess."

"Can you be more specific?"

"More specific?"

"Yes, can you describe that feeling more?"

"Um, I guess I felt a kind of relief inside, like when I said it, something inside of me agreed with it."

"You felt an inner harmony of sorts?"

"Yeah, I guess so…yeah."

"Wonderful, isn't it?"

Jeremy certainly felt so. It was a vastly different feeling, one he wanted to have more often. So, expressing gratitude seemed to be the way to achieve that. He wondered if there were other ways to feel relief inside.

With full stomachs, Jeremy was excited to get back on their way. He looked around the restaurant before they left to take it all in one more time. As they headed to the door, Jeremy noticed an adjacent room to his right with a door half ajar. He had a sense of adventure and curiosity that would have been ridiculed and attacked in his community, but this was perfectly acceptable and even encouraged here. He loved opportunities to express it, and this was another one. The term, "inspired action," came to mind.

He walked to the room and stepped just inside

the opening. There were several stages full of various characters with strings heading up and out of sight from where Jeremy stood. Each character tried to resist the strings' directions, but every time, they succumbed to the strings' wishes. Each character was redirected by the will of whomever manipulated the strings. The characters seemed calm at one moment, but with a pull of the strings, they became mad, furious even. Other times, a pull of a string animated them with joy and happiness.

"Ah yes, happy, mad, glad, sad—all the emotions being acted out because they are acted upon," Laluna said. If one doesn't live one's own life, then whose life is being lived?"

"They seem to be acting out whenever the strings are pulled," Jeremy replied. "Why don't they break away from what's manipulating them?"

"Why indeed? No one would choose to be a slave to another, but it's interesting how one can find oneself pointing to others for one's emotions and actions. Wouldn't emotional servitude be the worst kind? Giving one's mind to another. Being beholden to another for one's actions and state of wellbeing."

"Again, why don't they just break away?"

"They have chosen to play a role in another's play, rather than star in their own. They have handed who they are to another and know no other way. Another way takes an awareness of what's within, healing and strengthening what's within to break the ties that bind. Maybe a willingness that they just don't have and a fear they allow to hold them as they are. But whose life is it? Should it not be theirs to live?"

"How can they not be willing to change this terrible situation they are in?"

"We have found the challenge of change to be powerful for some, haven't we? What accumulates within can be hard to change and hard to be aware of. Of course, there's the forces of others, how accustomed they have become to who we are in their plays. We change characters on them, and it becomes a chaos they aren't prepared for."

"Well, it's not our fault they can't deal with it, right? They should just deal with it and be OK with it."

"It certainly isn't. What a line to walk between being mindful of our impact on others and allowing others to dictate how we live our lives."

Jeremy thought back to the fights with his mother. Why couldn't she just be happy for him? Why couldn't she just appreciate that he was different, that he was destined for more than just being a Reactor or an Insensor? Was she just afraid? Was she just too used to how he was and things were? Jeremy felt an emotion that crept up on him before. What was it? Compassion?

Laluna's question rang in his head: Who's life is it?

*It's my life,* he thought. *I can be mindful of my impact, but I have to live my life the way I feel I need to. That's why I left!*

Every Reactor is beholden to other people's reactions. That's part of the nature of things where he's from. Had he been a puppet in someone else's play? He accumulated all his experiences and bore the weight of them. His reactions have been driven by those around him. He feels beholden to what comes up from within. This all seemed overwhelming to him, but there was hope. He left. He took inspired and massive action. He is on his way to the mountain, and he feels sure, no matter how many have come before and have fallen short, that he will be successful.

# AGILITY

Laluna and Jeremy left the restaurant and Fujala to continue their journey toward the mountain, which seemed closer and clearer than ever. The weight of the rocks in Jeremy's bag was much lighter. Would the baggage of his past really shed as Laluna suggested? Now, he could take fuller strides, and his straightening body reached toward the sky.

Laluna noticed Jeremy's smile. "Such a journey you've had, my friend," she said. "As the weight of existence shifts within, so will your experiences shift around you."

"I can't wait to tell Them what I've found on my journey," Jeremy said with an excited tone in his voice. "They can finally tell me what They won't tell others, but I can also tell Them what They might not know,"

"Indeed! Sharing your knowledge and experience can be an amazing feeling, can't it?"

Jeremy wasn't sure he knows what that feels like because what has he actually known? And who would have listened anyway? He felt as if a thousand layers were removed from his eyes on this short, extensive journey. Leaving his community seems like a lifetime ago.

"Oh, goodness me, it is getting late, isn't it?" Laluna asked. "I can leave you in good hands for the night, my friend, and we can commence in the morning. How does that sound?"

"I guess you're right, but can't you stay?" Jeremy asked. "You're the only person I know here."

"Oh, my friend, just down the path, there is a friend who is a wondrous person, kind and thoughtful like no other. You will so enjoy him."

"But it will be awkward. What will I possibly say? What will we talk about? Will I have my own room? Privacy is important to me. Will there be food for me to eat? I only have so much with me. Oh, maybe I can head back to my house. No, it's too far now. What should I do?"

"You should breathe, my friend."

"Breathe? That's your answer? Breathe?"

"You so admired the skill our friend had when the fairies were buzzing about. You also saw that poor atomete keep turning away from what appeared to be nothing, only to make more attempts, and falling ever shorter of its goal. How we live in the future through anxiety, don't we? Imagined futures that are never to be. Creating fear for ourselves where none is needed. May I mention again, we live in the wreckage of our future by denying ourselves the joy of our moments. Have you come to trust me, my friend?"

"Well, yes, I guess I have."

"Do you think I would knowingly cause you harm?"

"No, I don't think you would."

"Have you not come this far so far?"

"I have, haven't I?"

"What will be, will be, but as you build resilience within, you…"

"Learn, adapt, and improve," Jeremy interrupted with a triumphant tone.

"Yes, my friend. That's exactly right. You learn, adapt, and improve because you are emotionally and intellectually agile."

"Emotionally and intellectually agile?"

"Yes, the more we achieve, the more experiences we allow in our lives, and the more we don't succumb to the fear that can be used to energize us, the more we are able to adapt to changes that come our way. We can emotionally adapt and intellectually shift to whatever happens around us, because we see it is happening only around us and not to us. Therein lies our choices to move forward positively."

"I have experienced a lot so far, haven't I?"

"More than you would have imagined!"

"Certainly! Much more! I have lived more today than I have in the years before."

"So, for what comes next, you feel more prepared than you have before because you've lived more than you have before."

"Yeah, I guess you're right."

"That is resilience building within you. Strength comes by working through resistance. Without resistance, there is no growth, but through resistance, resilience is instilled, and the more we can achieve."

"OK, let's go meet your friend. I'm ready," Jeremy said with a newfound confidence.

Jeremy and Laluna followed the path to Laluna's friend's house. Jeremy thought back to his community. It felt like a million miles away and a lifetime ago. He could feel himself getting closer to the mountain even more than he could see it getting closer. What would They tell him? What more is there?

# WHO ARE WE REALLY

Jeremy and Laluna walked for some time down the twists and turns of the path they had chosen. It was dusk, but Jeremy could still clearly see the amazing surroundings this new land provided. As they rounded another corner, he noticed a village to his left down a small path.

"Maybe we can take a moment and explore the village before finishing our day?" Jeremy asked.

"Well, sure, we have time, given we are nearly there already, Laluna replied. Let's see what's happening in Feldora with all the feldorians."

*Feldorians?* Jeremy wondered what sort of characters they would be. He had seen more than he could imagine so far. He felt more curiosity and excitement to explore than ever before. He wanted to consume these amazing experiences to build more of—what did Laluna call it? Oh yes, resilience. Exposing himself to new experiences would build that muscle she talked about and create those new memories, resulting in more positive thoughts. He wanted to be emotionally and intellectually agile. He knew now, or at least accepted, that he could do it.

They followed the short path to the edge of the village and paused to take in the activity. Feldora was bustling. Jeremy wasn't quite sure what was so different about feldorians. They looked average at first glance.

He saw one come out of her house and stop at a bin just outside the door. She rummaged through it, picking up masks and examining them. The masks almost resembled her face. Each mask was a variation of her own face, some closer and some much farther away from what she actually looked like. She quickly tried to find the one she was looking for, but it wasn't clear what her criteria was or that she had a specific goal in mind. As if by chance, the one she wanted appeared, she affixed it to her face seamlessly, and off she went. Jeremy couldn't see how the mask was fastened to her face.

He scanned the other homes in the village and saw similar activity from others. Each feldorian stopped outside their houses, picked a mask that had varying levels of similarity to themselves from a bin, and went on their way.

"Why are they putting on masks?" Jeremy asked.

"Ah, why indeed?" Laluna replied. How stressful it is to try and be someone you're not. The cause of so much discontent, so much misery, driven by showing up to others as someone you simply are not. What disasters can follow."

Jeremy watched as the newly-masked feldorians went about their lives. But as they interacted with others, he noticed their skin radiate energy as if it were coming from within and being expelled. Each pulse of energy caused physical pain. The feldorians winced and hunched over as if they were suspended from motion momentarily.

The feldorians' skin reflected the consequences of the energy pulses. It wrinkled and turned an ashy color. One after another, the feldorians returned to their respective bins and rummaged through them, desperately trying to find a replacement mask. Each seemed to find one and quickly replaced the current mask on their faces with the new ones. Jeremy noticed that some chose masks closer to their likeness, and others were far removed from their natural presence. The consequences from choosing a mask that closely represented themselves became clear: The energy was much stronger the farther away the mask was from the feldorians' true natures.

Those wearing masks that more closely matched their true appearance were mostly unaffected by the mild pulses, and some felt no pulses at all. These patterns continued, desperate attempts at finding various masks that would, well, Jeremy wasn't sure what the goal was. He was, however, desperately afraid of what he saw next.

One of the feldorians, who wore a mask vastly different from its true facade, was interacting with a small group of feldorians. Another small group approached and was, at first, coaxing the feldorian away from those he interacted with. The coaxing became more insistent, until the group tried to pull him away. The feldorian resisted, but the pulses coming from within increased in their ferocity, apparently weakening his will to resist. The feldorian's resistance waned and…

"No! You need to get away!" Jeremy's voice was barely audible from his fear inside.

Jeremy watched the thin line that separated the mask from the face it held disappear. It was no longer a mask; it simply was the feldorian. When the metamorphosis ended, the feldorian's resistance relinquished. He turned away from what was and left with what appeared to be his fate.

Jeremy turned to Laluna with a shocked look on his face.

"I have too many questions to know where to begin," was all Jeremy could manage to say.

"Yes, it is a challenge to see what we put ourselves through isn't it?" Laluna asked. "We want so desperately for others to see us a certain way, perceive us, receive us as we want them to. Our personas that we have at our disposal to portray the identities we think will create the life we want never do. It is only our true selves that will do."

"Personas and identities, what do you mean?"

"We are all different in different situations, so it is natural to be so. It is important, however, to be aligned with who one truly is inside. Departing too much creates intense internal tension, a kind of inner disconnection. An immense amount of energy is spent in the wrong direction. All of this causes terrible cycles with equally terrible consequences. One must know oneself first. One must be able to recognize the good and not so good masks we have at our disposal and be aware of which we put on at which time and the consequences to those decisions. But, alas, hardly a decision at times when we do so without awareness."

"You mean, knowing the light and the dark?" Jeremy asked quietly, thinking back to the laimenters.

"Ah, yes my friend, exactly that," Laluna replied with admiration.

"Because we have to take the time to know ourselves; otherwise, we are a calamity in our lives. Is that what happened to those feldorians?" Jeremy asked, motioning to those who succumbed to the intrusion of their masks.

"Why, yes, my friend, that's exactly right. Knowing oneself, truly knowing oneself, can release the tension within. One will have something to turn to when questions arise, an inner standard of sorts to help bring light to even the darkest circumstances."

"It is a journey. That's what you said. I'm on a journey now to find out what They don't tell us. Maybe I don't know myself as well as I need to in order to make the changes They are going to share with me. But I feel different."

Jeremy looked at his dwindling bag of rocks and stretched his back. It was almost straight now. He took a deep breath.

"I am finding so much along my way here," he continued. "I am collecting more but shedding an equal amount, but none of the new is weighing me down."

"As we learn about ourselves and start to act in accordance with those discoveries, we can bear the weight of our own existence with ease," Laluna said. "How free we become! We can then start to resolve those inner disconnections and show up authentically in all situations we face."

The weight of our own existence, that was it! His mother, his father, his so-called friend, they were succumbing to their own existence, a weight they could hardly bear. Was becoming an Insensor what one wants or just what one accepts to become? Is this like the fate of that feldorian and the atomete? It seemed they were simply compelled toward action instead of taking action with intention. Yes! That's what it is, intention. Even the atometes were calamities, a consequence of the pneumon's reactions.

Achieving harmony with what's within and discovering who one truly is, accepting what is within, allows one to live with intention. One must live their life, not someone else's life. One must live a life of intention.

"We should make our way, my friend," Laluna said. "It is nearly dark and we have a bit to go before reaching Peruma's house."

They continued in silence as Jeremy reflected on his journey. He witnessed more throughout this day than in all the years he lived. It was overwhelming. Maybe fatigue was taking over. Whatever it was, he was looking forward to arriving at Peruma's house and getting some much needed rest.

# BEING WILLING TO ACCEPT

Before they knew it, they had arrived. Peruma's house was humble but nice, with plant life around it and brightly colored walls to match the surrounding exuberance. Jeremy was looking forward to relaxing after an incredibly complex and amazing day, but just as fast as those thoughts entered his mind, they were pushed out by the sounds of a party. Jeremy could feel his apprehension build as his anxiety returned, slowing his progress toward the house. Laluna noticed Jeremy's apprehension and placed her hand on his shoulder.

"You have learned to lean into these experiences," she said. "It can be that much more difficult when our strength is worn from fatigue, but it is still within you to accept that these are the moments that growth happens. There is no growth without resistance. Just as our muscles require it to grow, so our mental core requires it, too. Be willing to accept the emotions that reveal themselves. No oppression. No suppression. Not even control, but a willing acceptance and then perseverance."

Jeremy knew Laluna was right. He closed his eyes, picturing that amazing man they saw in the field of fairies earlier today. He thought about that serene state the man was able to achieve regardless of the chaos around him and the joy Laluna found in that very chaos. Jeremy had come this far. Why not go further?

With his eyes opened, Jeremy turned his anxiety into the energy necessary to propel him forward. They both walked to the door with confidence and knocked loudly in hopes that Peruma could hear them over the music playing inside.

Peruma answered the door with a smile. "Welcome, my friends! So good to see you, Laluna. And who is this?"

"This is my friend Jeremy," Laluna said. "He has come a long way and is headed to the mountain. We were hoping he could stay here tonight and continue the journey tomorrow."

"Oh, the mountain, you say? This is much farther than I have seen such travelers. I can imagine how weary you must be, how much the experiences have made their impression."

Other such travelers? Jeremy thought. There it is again. The others must not have traveled to this point. Has he come farther than the others?

"Come in! Come in!" Peruma said. "We have food, drink, music, and lots of amazing people to meet. Everyone is having the best time. No worries here! We leave them at the door!"

Peruma showed Laluna and Jeremy in and closed the door.

Jeremy was hesitant but saw the food and moved toward it. He was hungry from his day of travel. He quietly looked around and noticed everyone having a great time talking, eating, drinking, and dancing.

Laluna joined him by his side. "Are you going to meet some people?" she asked.

"Maybe. I'm going to eat something first and take

some time to get comfortable." Jeremy replied.

He barely finished those words when a rhythmic knocking at the door echoed through the house. Peruma's eyes seemed to explode out of his head. With a look of desperation, he rushed to the stereo, and turned the music off.

"Shhhh! Shhhh! Everyone! Shhhh!" Peruma repeated while flipping off the light switches.

Everyone immediately froze in place and waited in the silence and darkness for what would happen next. The rhythmic knocking resumed with a firmer hand.

"Go away! Peruma shouted. "There's nothing here for you!"

The knocking persisted. Then the door handle began to wiggle, which successfully released the door from its frame. Peruma ran to the door and managed to slam it shut before the intruder could widen the gap. He pressed against the door to hold it in place while the guests whispered in the background.

"Leave! I don't want you here! Just leave me alone!" Peruma shouted. The intruder attempted a few more nudges at the door, gave up, and retreated.

The whispers from the guests changed to murmurs, and the looks on their faces were clear: they were confused and disheartened. They were no longer in the mood to party.

"Who was at the door? Do you know?" Jeremy asked while the guests grabbed their belongings and headed to the door.

Before Laluna could answer, Peruma pleaded, "Friends, friends, don't go! Let's get back to the party! Plenty of fun to be had still." He turned on the lights and stereo, but this didn't encourage the guests to stay. They left in silence with uncomfortable smiles—their only compensation for Peruma's efforts.

"With all that is good around us, we stop it to focus on that one thing that we perceive as negative, sacrificing all that is positive," Laluna said.

"Well, whoever was at the door ruined the party," Jeremy said.

"Did they, or was the reaction to them what ruined the party? Could they have really been so terrible as to have a worse outcome than what we see now?"

"I guess you're right. Maybe if Peruma just let whoever it was in, he could have handled it, and people might not even have noticed."

"So much arises within and happens around us. We label it as negative when it is only that label that gives it meaning. So often, what is, is simply what it is—information, an occurrence to experience. The more we resist, attempt to control, or oppress, the more we take away from all the good that is happening within and around us. This is what is meant by willingness to accept. Be willing to accept what comes and allow it to pass, never to let it sweep you away."

Jeremy thought back to the atometes that fought with their internal pneumons and the troggles being swept away by those fiery red creatures. How often has he tried to control whatever came from within him instead of just letting it be what it is, accepting and letting it pass on by? How often did he let what comes from within sweep him away in his moments, driving reactions as the Reactor he thought he was?

"Everything passes by us," Laluna continued. "All that is, is transient, simply momentary. Why get so caught up in any single thought, emotion, event, when the memory of it will be beyond our reach soon enough? The most intense moments become a distant memory before long. Imagine yourself zooming out from the intensity, projecting yourself into the future, and looking back. How small it would seem."

It is true. Jeremy thought. He can remember so many times in his life that a thought came to mind, an emotion swept over him, his mother spoke harsh words, so many things that simply came and went. Does he even remember? The substance of those moments are gone. All that remains is a sense they might have occurred and the understanding that being so caught up with what was seems silly in the present moment.

"Oh, so glad you're still here," Peruma said. "We can have our own party, can we not? Who needs them anyway?"

"My friend Peruma, I must be going, and Jeremy has had quite the day" Laluna said. "We are so thankful for your hospitality and would love to join your future gatherings as they are such great fun." She looked at Jeremy in hopes of encouraging a response from him.

"Oh, um, yeah, it has been a long day, sir," Jeremy said. "I'd really appreciate it if I could get some rest and continue my journey first thing in the morning. And, um, I'm sorry that your party didn't go as you had hoped."

Jeremy felt something within, something similar to his thought about his father earlier that day on the way to class. He pushed the feeling away at the time, but allowed it to flow through him this time and drive his response to the situation. It felt good! Was this the compassion that Laluna referred to?

"My dear boy, I do appreciate that," Peruma said. "Come, come, let me show you to your room where you can rest for your journey forward tomorrow."

Jeremy turned to Laluna. He hesitated. This will be the first time he will be away from her, his companion since he entered this new world.

Laluna smiled. "I will be back first thing, and we will continue. I wouldn't miss your next steps for the world."

Her words comforted Jeremy. He looked at Peruma, showing that he was ready. He followed Peruma down a hallway to a nice, quaint bedroom. Jeremy was thankful to find a separate bathroom and what looked like a very comfortable bed. He didn't want to counteract his compassionate expression earlier with anything that could be perceived as rude, but he was ready for quiet and some alone time. Fortunately, Peruma was prepared to leave him to escort Laluna to the door.

"Well, there you go, young man," Peruma said. "Please let me know if you need anything. I won't be but a call away." He whisked himself out the door, shutting it behind him.

At last, a peaceful moment for Jeremy to collect his thoughts. He washed up and crawled into bed. He stared at the ceiling, thinking back to the morning where he had done the same, imagining something different, something more for himself. And, here he was, a light year away from there, an eon away from that moment. He had come so far, but still not far enough. He wanted to get to the mountain and really find out what They don't tell others in his community. What do They know that others don't?

He began to think back through all that he witnessed today. As the first thoughts entered his mind, they were overcome quickly with the heaviness of his eyes, which surrendered to sleep.

# Patience and Humility

Jeremy's eyes popped open after one of the best night's sleeps he's ever had. He felt invigorated for the day ahead. He noticed that his anxiety, or rather, the feeling he normally had within him, wasn't the same. It was more just an excited energy. Sure, he felt anxious, but all he had been through the previous day told him that he could take on today, no matter what it brought. He started to understand what Laluna meant by emotionally and intellectually agile. The resilience he never had within seemed to be growing moment by moment. He bounded out of bed, quickly dressed, and headed out of the room and down the hall.

When Peruma saw Jeremy, he greeted Jeremy with, "Ah, good morning! Would you like to join us for breakfast?" Peruma motioned Jeremy to the table where Laluna was already enjoying the food he prepared.

"I trust you slept well, my friend," Laluna said. "You certainly look well rested and ready for your day."

"I did sleep well, thank you." Jeremy said, as he took a seat and dove right into the wonderful food laid out for him.

"This is really nice of you to help us, letting Jeremy stay here and giving us such great food,"

Laluna said to Peruma, looking at Jeremy to agree with her.

"Oh, yeah, um, thanks Peruma. It's really great!" Jeremy said.

"Thank you, my friends. I won't be but a moment," Peruma said as he left the kitchen.

"Isn't it great to show not only the compassion you did last night, but the gratitude we showed just now?" Laluna asked Jeremy. "It is a gift we can always give to another as we talked before about giving it to ourselves. It lifts us up and others. It is the antidote for so many of our ailments. If we simply take the time to be grateful of what we have, who we are, and who we have in our lives, what is within becomes that much more positive."

Jeremy thought back to their previous conversation. Being grateful for the little things as well as the big things in life did seem to make him feel better. Showing compassion as he did in the previous night and expressing gratitude as he just did seem to evoke similar feelings within him. But It helps with what's within? Maybe that place within himself, the source of the negative he feels needs that to move toward being positive. But how to do what she describes? Maybe just looking for more opportunities to express both?

He was anxious to get going on the day, so he left that thought. He was hoping to reach the mountain early enough so he could learn from Them and head back to his community before sundown.

"Do you think we could get going soon?" Jeremy asked. "The mountain is getting so close. It seems like we could get there soon, don't you think?"

"Sure, my friend. We have an amazing day ahead

of us. Let's say our goodbyes and start on our way."

Peruma returned. "Oh, you must be on your way," he said. "No time to lose. So proud to see another, especially someone this far along. Laluna, you truly are wonderful, aren't you? So good at what you do. So much ahead for you, my new friend. I must be getting to my shop. I'm short on help and have much to do."

"Oh, thank you so much, my friend," Laluna said. "It has been an amazing journey so far, and I'm so thankful that Jeremy let me come along. OK, Jeremy, let's get on our way."

"Yeah, thanks again, Peruma," Jeremy said. "I'd say I'll see you again, but once I find what I've come to find, I'll be taking it back to my community, but I do appreciate you letting me stay with you and giving me food to start my day."

*This gratitude thing is getting easier and easier,* Jeremy thought.

"Oh, sharing what you find. What a wonderful thing to do," Peruma said while they all walked to the door. "That is when it will truly all come together for you."

They left the house, Jeremy and Laluna going one way and Peruma going another.

"Be well, my friend," Laluna said as they departed.

"We are as good as we see the world to be, aren't we?" Peruma replied, as he hustled on his way.

"Indeed we are," Laluna said.

"Laluna, Peruma mentioned others more than once," Jeremy said. "Have you helped other people from my community? How far did they get? What did they find? It seems like they didn't make it to the mountain. Peruma said I've come farther than others. Is that true?"

"Patience and humility, the two most overlooked and underappreciated attributes one can possess," Laluna replied. "I want to share and be honest with you. What if I told you that accepting not knowing the answer to that helps you to achieve what you are after here? Would you trust in that?"

Jeremy thought about this. He knew the previous version of himself would never accept being put off as Laluna was clearly doing, but what would the new Jeremy do? Patience and humility, what did those words mean in this context?

"So, if I'm patient and trust in what you're saying, that will help me to get to the mountain and learn from Them?" Jeremy asked.

"Humility to accept we don't know everything and patience to acquire the knowledge that is to come," Laluna replied. "Yes, my friend, this is what I find to be true. It can be challenging for some. Too often, we want to hurry on our way to success. We want to know everything, and we want to know it now, but can one know everything? I think not. Being curious, seeking to understand, but having the patience to recognize that knowledge comes when we are ready to receive it. So often, we experience things that we don't see. We are blinded by what we drag into those situations, denying ourselves the lesson."

"Is this related to the wise learner the tree mentioned?"

"In a way it is, yes. Patience to know life has an ebb and flow to it and humility to accept what others know that we might not. What a powerful combination."

"OK, I'll trust you." Those words had such an amazing effect on Jeremy, not too dissimilar from the new sensations he had been experiencing since leaving his community. Trusting in another was as unfamiliar as the characters he had encountered so far on his journey and the experiences he's had along his way, but it felt good. It felt right.

# THE MOUNTAIN

What a start to Jeremy's day! It hadn't been long since he opened his eyes, but he had already learned so much. He could see the mountain so close now. He felt sure they would be there in no time. He started to envision meeting Them and what he'd say. He wouldn't be demanding. He'd learn better about that. He'd show them humility and patience, as Laluna explained to him. That will definitely get Them to open up to him and tell him what They don't tell others.

Just as these thoughts settled in, they arrived at a clearing. Jeremy took a deep breath, as the scope of what was happening in this large area in front of them was overwhelming. He searched for a place to make some sense of things and found what looked like the genesis of it all. In the far left extreme of the clearing, he saw a swirl of dust form into a mini tornado. The swirling seemed to have a purpose, Jeremy noticed, when a humanoid creature appeared from the dust.

"Oh! What an incredible find we've stumbled upon," Laluna said. "The diggits make their way from start to finish but not without the fortines directing who they become as they follow their cycles, well, at least most of them."

Jeremy looked back at the diggits walking in a straight line from where they started. He looked closer at them and realized they shared a trait with the atometes

"They have a pneumon inside of them like the atometes," Jeremy said.

"Sure! Whether it is visible or not, don't we all have something working on our behalf?" Laluna asked. "In fact, more than we like to realize is done on our behalf. We are simply unaware. But we have faced this before, my friend. To become who we want to be, we must work with, feed properly, train, and collaborate with what's within. We do so, mindfully empowering ourselves with intention, to respond to our lives with that intention."

As the diggits walked in their initial straight line, the fortines came up to them, bringing what looked like a ball of energy cradled in their hands. It reminded Jeremy of the pneumons when they created the ball of energy within the atometes. He thought about how that energy directed the atometes and impacted the others around them.

Like the energy in the atometes, the fortines' energy was of different colors, shapes, and intensities. The variations were endless among them. The fortines projected the ball of energy into an opening on top of the diggits' heads that was as wide as the heads would allow. Jeremy saw the energy spread through a network that ran throughout the diggits' bodies. But all the energy headed to two destinations: the pneumon and a small, solid mass at the center of the diggits, just above where the pneumon resided. Both the pneumon and this mass changed with each burst of energy. The pneumon changed in color, size, and intensity in proportion to the energy, and the mass within the diggits increased in size, but Jeremy couldn't distinguish any changes beyond that.

"You might have noticed the addition of the diggits' mental core within them that lives alongside the pneumons," Laluna said. "What an important part of how one shows up in one's life. As our physical strength, stability, and balance comes from those muscles within us, so does the strength, stability, and balance of our responses come from the mental core. The stronger it is, the stronger we are. The healthier it is, the healthier we respond."

After a series of these energy bursts, each diggit started following various paths, each of which seemed predestined. It was difficult for Jeremy to take all of this in and track all the different diggits. Much as before, he focused his attention on individual diggits to see what would unfold. He saw one going into an area of the clearing and momentarily lying on a bed, getting up, walking to a table, sitting down, standing up, walking to a desk, sitting down, standing up, turning around and returning to the table, sitting down, standing up, and heading back to the bed where it started. If that wasn't strange enough, a moment later, the diggit repeated that exact sequence!

What Jeremy saw inside the diggits was as confusing as anything he had witnessed so far. The pneumon projected a ball of energy, the same as they did with the atometes Jeremy saw yesterday. The energy went through the mental core and emerged from the other side with a different color and intensity than it had entered with. Then another energy source moved down from the diggits' heads to meet the energy coming from the diggits' mental cores. Next, the energy combined into a single surge. This combination of energy was responsible for the repetitive cycles these diggits were following and any other mindless actions they took.

"We believe what we are aware of drives our decisions in life," Laluna said. "We believe that we choose our actions freely, but so much is done on our behalf well before we become aware and make a decision. What's within serves us what it believes it must to continue the patterns we follow. This, combined with what we have known before—the patterns and memories we have lived—is what primes us to respond to our life as we always have."

"But why?" Jeremy asked. "Why does it want to keep us in those patterns?"

"To protect us. To keep us small and safe, to live an unimagined life without risk. What an ancient instinct that has served us well, but now holds us hostage in our own lives."

Along this repetitive journey, the fortines periodically approached the diggits and projected energy bursts through the diggits' openings on their heads, but Jeremy noticed that the openings became smaller and smaller, allowing fewer and fewer energy bursts in. The expression of the diggits was blank. They followed a habitual pattern and surrendered to what the fortines projected onto them.

This shocked Jeremy initially, but then the thoughts of his father came to mind. In fact, thoughts of all the Insensors came to mind. Were the Insensors of his community just a byproduct of the situations they faced, carrying their bag of rocks along their journey of life? For what? What was it all for? Does he just follow patterns or cycles in his life? It was the same, day in and day out, just bearing the weight of his existence. Well, that was the case until he left his community behind. But so many others were stuck in that same cycle he was before.

"It is remarkable how closed off we become to new experiences when they have only been imposed on us, rather than intentionally sought and accepted," Laluna said. "Growth stops, and we have stopped living before our lives are over."

Jeremy turned his attention back to the scene and watched more repeated patterns play out. One diggit sat at a desk, stood up, and walked to a machine. The diggit pushed a button, and money came out of the machine. Then the diggit turned around, walked to a fire, and threw the money in the fire! The diggit then went back and did exactly the same thing! Yet another diggit repeated this pattern but took the money and threw it into a hole outside the house it lived in. Jeremy watched this pattern repeat several times, but at some point the diggit returned to its house without any money. This repeated a couple of times until a fortine stood in front of the diggit as it returned to its house and the diggit was turned away. Another diggit then took the original diggit's place. This new diggit replaced the previous diggit's pattern. Each of the diggits seemed to be driven by the combination of energy coming from its head, the pneumon, and filtering from the mental core within.

"What is happening here?" Jeremy asked. "This all seems quite terrible. They seem miserable." Jeremy hoped for some guidance from Laluna to understand what he was seeing.

"So often, we passively accept the misery in our lives," Laluna said. She reached out and held Jeremy's arm to get his attention. It worked. They locked gazes, and Laluna repeated herself.

"We passively accept the misery in our lives. Pain is inevitable, but misery is a choice. It is a choice made to accept it as part of our lives or move beyond it. We can be victims in our lives or legends. It is our choice."

"They don't look like they are choosing anything," Jeremy said.

"Ah, yes, the habitual patterns of life. Doesn't it seem those you see here are a consequence of what is given to them, the by-product of what was done to them and around them? It is interesting how those patterns become the life that's followed, the life that's lived."

"So, there's no way for them to make a better choice for themselves?"

"Choices can only be made if you are aware of them, and you can only be aware of them if you are aware of what's within. Otherwise, you are simply a calamity in life."

There's that word again, calamity. Was he a calamity in his own life? Jeremy thought about the characters with strings attached to them, directing their movements. Has he been living his life or other people's lives? Are the diggits living their lives or what the fortines direct them to live? Or is the pneumon within driving them? What about the mental core inside of them? Everything within them started from what was imposed on them from the outside. So, was he a calamity? Was he just a consequence of his circumstances? The word, *intention*, came back to his mind. Were the diggits living with intention? Was he living with intention? Had he passively accepted the misery in his life? Had he passively accepted his circumstances and not recognized the choices he had?

Jeremy felt his anxiety return, gnawing at him as he reflected on the limitations he now started to feel were imposed on his life. Could he use his anxiety? Is the anxiety he felt really his? What did Laluna say? "It's just what's within, giving you a warning that something needs to change and there's something to pay attention to." Well, there was a lot to pay attention to. Jeremy decided to use that energy to refocus his attention on the scene at hand and discover more from it.

While he did this, Jeremy noticed the first gleam of hope he'd seen. One of the diggits in an impossible cycle stopped, and as the two sources of energy inside it came together, the diggit reached within and pulled the energy out with intention. The diggit held it in its hands, examined it, and then tossed it aside where it immediately dissipated. The diggit started to take steps in a different direction, and as it did, it brought its hands together and a new ball of energy formed. The diggit then fed that energy into the hole previously thought to be reserved for the fortines. The energy did what it had done earlier—changing the pneumon and the mental core within the diggit, but now that change was different. The pneumon became lighter, with a gentle radiance. The mental core became more transparent and less differentiated from the body in which it resided.

Fortines approached this diggit again, but the diggit stopped them. The diggit's response prevented the fortines from depositing the energy they carried. Instead of simply passively accepting what came to it, the diggit sought what it wanted with intention.

This awakened diggit approached the fortines instead of waiting to be approached. It chose what it wanted and didn't want, taking the energy from the fortines it preferred and depositing the energy into itself. Jeremy noticed the hole widen to receive more of the diggit's newfound energy. The diggit's expression changed from blank to driven.

"Is that what you were talking about before, living with intention?" Jeremy asked.

"Why yes, my friend, it certainly appears to be an example of not simply accepting what comes from within nor simply accepting what comes from the external, but to intentionally choose how to engage in life. How else does one break the cycles they follow?"

Jeremy continued to see more diggits experience a similar awakening. They were intercepting the energy and redirecting it toward what served their newfound drive. What was even more striking was that some of the diggits went to others and intercepted the fortines' attempts at projecting the energy as they had done before. The diggits that helped in this way created their own energy and fed it to the diggit they were helping until the diggit could do it for itself.

The pneumons continued to send their energy up through the mental core, but the mental core within the awakened diggits continued to be more transparent, less differentiated. The energy that left was lighter, brighter, more brilliant, and the energy that came from above matched that brilliance. Once the energy combined, it was even more brilliant.

"Ah yes, finding purposeful meaning in their lives," Laluna said.

"What did you say?" Jeremy asked in an excited but shocked tone.

"Well, purposeful meaning is what life's successes are all about, isn't it?"

Jeremy couldn't believe his ears! Laluna said one of the phrases he found in the book from the library, the book that started his journey. How did she know that phrase? What did it mean? He teemed with excitement. He might be closer to knowing what They don't tell others than he thought!

"Do you know what purposeful meaning means?" Jeremy blurted out.

"Well, purpose is intent and meaning is value, so it is the intended value you have for your life," Laluna replied. "What do you see when you see those diggits?" She pointed at the diggits that were helping the others.

"I see them helping the other diggits."

"Sure. Would you say they are adding value to their fellow diggits' lives?"

"It certainly seems so. The diggits they are helping are better off, for sure."

"Imagine adding value to others is how you live your life every day. Imagine that's what drives you and your decisions. Imagine it is just who you are at your core, someone who wants to help and add value to others and be the best you can be. That, my friend, is living."

"An Optimal Life?"

"Why yes, my friend, an Optimal Life indeed."

The epiphany nearly knocked Jeremy off his feet. He had traveled so far to find others that could tell him the meaning of those words, but the meaning came to him when he was ready to receive it.

Jeremy's gaze returned to the awakened diggits continuing their transformations. If this represented what he had discovered, he wanted all of the attention he could muster. He felt a mindful focus set in. He knew more about what that word meant now, in this moment.

Now, there was harmony between what the pneumons produced and what was coming from the head of the diggits. The mental core in the diggits enhanced the brightness and even changed the dark energy to light energy at times. The diggits used that energy to continue to propel themselves toward the destination they strived for. When any diggits struggled, others stepped in and helped, especially when a fortine tried to impose its energy on a diggit making its way toward something Jeremy couldn't identify.

"Where are they going?" Jeremy asked.

"Well, each to their own, my friend," Laluna replied. "Success is quite individual but found through quite the same means. It is the Optimal Life, the state of being we achieve when we have found harmony with what was and what's within. We respond to our lives instead of reacting, and we live with intention. We align with who we truly are inside, our authentic self. We have relieved ourselves of the inner tension that comes from being someone we aren't. We show up consistent for ourselves. We add value to others and are ready to receive value back."

As Jeremy looked around, he could still see the mountain ever closer in his sight. The mountain's shadow reached to the scene in front of them. It seemed to be in multiple places at once, as if offering itself to anyone willing to meet it.

As the diggits moved toward their destinations, they walked the path the mountain's shadow gave to them. It was as if they had found their own mountains when they started to walk with intention in their lives.

Jeremy looked just beyond where he stood and saw the tip of the mountain's shadow just a few steps away. He stepped forward, but it receded. He took another step, and the recession continued. His confused eyes, with a hint of fear, looked at Laluna for an answer.

"It is so important to leave what was where it belongs to truly move toward the life we deserve," Laluna said. "Too often we drag the baggage of our past into our moments, denying ourselves the future we deserve. Once inner clarity is reached, once we truly know ourselves, we can draw our line, step over it, and move forward, leaving what was where it belongs."

Laluna's gaze fell on Jeremy's bag of rocks, now much smaller than before, but still held tightly by Jeremy.

"I was taught that what was will always be," Jeremy said. "I don't see how that can possibly be true."

"Indeed, my friend. Maybe what was is just what was, but what will be is what you make it to be. Everyone's definition of success for their lives is different, but what's common is to heal and strengthen your mental core, to find peace and connection with what's within, to find purposeful meaning, and to respond to your life with intention. We either set ourselves free of what was, or we don't. It is a choice. Life is challenging enough. Why bear the weight of the past that doesn't serve us any longer?"

Laluna glanced at Jeremy's bag of rocks, then motioned to the diggits that clearly had different destinations. All of these destinations were aligned with the shadows of the mountain.

*She's right,* Jeremy thought. *Everything has changed for me. I feel different. I am different. What was simply is what was, but what will be is up to me.*

Jeremy looked at his bag of rocks, the tip of the mountain's shadow, and the diggits achieving their successes. He felt a momentary peace within him as he looked again at his bag of rocks, wanting to ease his grip on it. He felt his anxiety return and turned to Laluna.

"I'm feeling a bit of anxiety within me," Jeremy said. "I think that means I need to act, as you said, lean into it, right?"

"Oh, my friend, you have it within you to do all you want to do, to achieve all you want to achieve," Laluna said.

"I think I know who They are. It isn't that They don't tell us, it's that we aren't listening to what others have to teach us and what is within us has to teach us. As the tree said, a wise learner learns something from everyone. Everyone is Them, and if we listen, then They can tell us all we need to know to live our Optimal Life. It is a matter of taking inspired action. It is a matter of accepting the temporary chaos of change, knowing that only through that chaos, we can live differently. When we live in our past, we deny ourselves our future, and the possibilities of our moments. It is time I leave the past where it belongs."

Jeremy took one last look at his bag of rocks as he gently, softly laid it on the ground. He took his final steps forward on his journey as the shadow of the mountain allowed him to overtake it.

# TRUE SUCCESS

Jeremy felt more change in that moment than he had felt in his entire life. He set out to travel to a mountain that came to him when he was ready. He wanted to find out what They didn't tell others, but found all of Them along his way. He sat where he stood, as if driven by a need to reflect on all that he had experienced. He closed his eyes. The sounds around him faded. He sensed his faithful companion, Laluna, join him. Her presence comforted him as he reflected on his journey.

There were so many lessons to absorb. Each one appeared as if it was confetti thrown for a celebration. He knew now not to attempt to suppress, oppress, or control the thoughts and emotions that came to him. He would observe them as if they were from another's mind's eye. He would be willing to accept what came to him in this moment. He wouldn't get swept away by any of it, but mindfully intervene with the intention to be curious and explore.

Jeremy began to let the thoughts flow through him: It is important to define success. It's hard to get somewhere if you don't know where that somewhere is. But success isn't a destination. It's a process. You hit milestones along your journey of life, achieving more clarity, a higher state of being. You find peace within and freedom from your past, which empowers you to live your life by your design. You've prepared to respond to your life, and you actually respond based on that preparation, with intention. You respond based on the standard within, not as others direct. You have to have a plan in life, a strategy to follow. You have to get started! The only way to move forward is to take action. Thoughts drive thinking, and thinking drives action. It is only through action that you create new experiences and can change how you live your life. You have to stay focused, but listen to others. Be a wise learner along your journey. Ask good questions to challenge yourself in your life, to make sure you stay directionally aligned to your success. Commit to yourself, and commit to others. Be patient with yourself and others. Conclusions and judgements are always premature. You'll never know more than those you judge and more information can empower you to draw better conclusions, which means you have to be open to challenge assumptions and conclusions. So much opportunity lives within those challenges.

Not only do you have to define success, but you have to discover yourself. you don't know yourself as well as you think you do or need to in order to make the changes you want to make. You are simply reacting to your life. Understanding the good within you as well as the not-so-good gives you the clarity to start healing what's within. What's within drives so much of your life. You can fight with it. You can try and oppress or suppress it. You can allow it to direct your life, but the more you do, the more it will limit you on your journey through life. It is listening to the whispers, getting in tune with what's within and using it to empower you forward. All of it is simply more to know, to be curious about. None of it needs to sweep you down the river of your life. The thought stream within might just be chatter, noise to be ignored, or information to ask questions of. To live mindfully is to have the power to keep what is useful and to let the rest pass right on by. You don't choose your thoughts. They simply make their appearance from within. Emotions follow along and can paralyze or energize. That is where your choice resides.

What you allow to feed what's within will drive what is served back to you. It is the stories you tell, the narratives that you weave within your minds that drive so much of how you show up in your life. It is your story to tell, your narrative to create. You might as well make it one that empowers you to live the life you want. When you allow others to feed what's within and direct how you show up in your life, you have given your life to another. You have become an emotional slave in your own life. Too often, you are a consequence or by-product of your experiences. Those experiences were imposed on you, making you a calamity in your own life. It is when you disrupt the patterns and push back on that imposition that you can start to live your life with intention and toward the success you deserve. What is within wants to protect you by looking to your past to warn you about your future, but this keeps you hostage to the habitual patterns of your life and denies you your potential. The path to living an Optimal Life is through mindfully intervening in these patterns to teach what's within how you want to live your life. It is through achieving inner clarity and peace. It is found by helping others to do the same. It is found by empowering yourself and others to create positive patterns based on a healthy and strong mental core and harmony with what's within.

What was his success? Jeremy thought it was getting to the mountain and finding out what They don't tell others. He learned that success was living an Optimal Life, but what does that mean to him? If everyone has different definitions for success, then what was his? Has he achieved it already? He felt his quiet being disrupted by the intrusion of those thoughts. His eyes opened, and his head turned to find Laluna, his faithful companion, already meeting his gaze with a reassuring smile.

"You have not come this far to only come this far, my friend," she said. "Success isn't a destination but a process. It is the process that we enjoy. You do know the final destination of life, right? Isn't it our lives that we enjoy, each moment that comprises it? You have become more than you were and will continue to refine what all this means to you."

"I'll learn, adapt, and improve?" Jeremy asked.

"Exactly! There's so much ahead of you. You have found the success you set out for, and there are more successes ahead of you. You will carry the lessons forward and take action toward living your Optimal Life."

"But where do I go from here? Where do we go from here?"

"What do you think are your next steps to take?"

"Well, I defined my success and took action toward it, but the finish line changed for me. But, like you said, we have to be emotionally and intellectually agile. Things change around us all the time."

"True! So often, what we thought would be, changes. It is what we do with the change, how we perceive it, and receive it that matters."

"I found the mountain I needed when I was ready to see it for what it was. I know that I don't need to find Them because They found me, or maybe I found Them as my journey went on. I guess there is no They, but just us. All of us are on our journeys and can teach each other a little bit through our encounters."

"It seemed to me that you were excited to find out what They don't tell others so you could bring it back to your community," Laluna recalled.

"True, but I wanted to do so to prove that I'm better than they are," Jeremy replied. "I wanted to show them I know more and am more than they are. That doesn't seem like part of success to me now."

"Why is that, my friend?"

"It seemed our diggit friends only found their true success when they helped others. Rubbing something in someone's face wouldn't help them. It only makes them feel bad about themselves. It wouldn't make me feel very good about myself, either."

"So, what do you think you could do instead?"

"Well, I want to show the people in my community that there is more to life than being a Reactor, that eventually, if they're 'lucky,' they can turn into an Insensor. Maybe I could make them see there is more to their lives. Maybe I could explain to them what I've learned, and they would want to live an Optimal Life." Jeremy's excitement grew when he thought about the possibilities awaiting him after he returned to his community.

"Remember our friends, the feldorians? They embraced the light and the dark. They discovered who they were inside and were excited to share those discoveries with others. Do you remember what happened?"

"Yeah, it seemed others didn't want to hear it and even attacked them over it. They didn't handle that rejection well."

"As we've seen, others have to live their lives, and you have to live yours. When our lives intersect, we bring our light and dark with us. We bring the past we haven't set down with us. We bring the patterns that we know with us. When you disrupt your patterns, even for the good, it can disrupt other people's patterns that they aren't ready to have disrupted."

"But I have to try, or rather, I will do what I can, and what I can do will be enough."

"And that's all we can do, my friend. Sometimes we have to just leave the clues of our success for others to find when they are ready. Success always leaves clues. We just have to be aware enough to recognize them."

"I feel like my journey has ended, but there's so much more to do at the same time. Does that even make sense?"

"Each end creates a beginning for us to explore. This is that moment for you."

"I think I want to head back to my community and share what I've found. I'm sure there is more to see from here back to there. As you said, I just have to pay attention, right?"

"Indeed, my friend. Let's see where it takes us." Laluna turned to start their journey.

# PERSIST FORWARD

Jeremy was still in deep reflection. There were so many lessons that were coming together for him. He was thinking about his family, his friends, his teachers—all those in his community who will be shocked by the fact they don't have to live as they are. They don't have to be Reactors or Insensors. There is more to life than dragging around a bag of rocks, seeking to accumulate more until there are no more days for them. That they can all shed the baggage of their past and move forward to live the life they want, an Optimal Life.

*Will they hear me?* he wondered, *Will they be like those the laimenter encountered after recognizing and accepting the light and the dark? That laimenter was rejected, ridiculed, and attacked for celebrating his discovery of himself.*

As soon as this thought arrived, Jeremy noticed that Laluna was taking a different path than the one that led them to the diggits and the path they arrived on.

"Laluna, you're going the wrong way," Jeremy said.

"What is the wrong way if what you seek is more than you know now?" she asked. "Do you remember what our friend, the tree, said to us?"

"That all paths lead to where we can be."

"Exactly! Where you were got you to where you

are but won't now get you to where you're going. The paths traveled will only give to us what we already have. We will seek paths to give us more and stretch us further."

Laluna continued to follow the alternate path.

Jeremy had trusted Laluna so much along their journey. What she said made so much sense, sense he doubts he would have found before this journey started.

They traveled for some time through the winding trails. There were more travelers to and from on this path than the previous ones taken. Most greeted Jeremy and Laluna with a smile, and some seemed to busily pass right on by. Jeremy took it all in stride. He felt he was on a celebratory walk back to his community. He was full of smiles, joy, and hope, but he felt doubt creep in off and on. Will those in his community hear his stories of discovery? Will they listen? He decided to say this to Laluna to see if she would reassure him or confirm his doubts.

"I can't wait to get back and share all I've learned with everybody in my community," Jeremy said.

"And how do you think that will go?" Laluna asked.

Jeremy paused briefly before saying, "I don't know. What do you think? Do you think it will go well?"

"Ah, my friend, I like that you are asking questions. No more are you just explaining and talking to what comes to mind, but exploring other people's perspectives. This is a skill that will certainly help when you make your triumphant return."

"How so?"

"The more we talk, the less others feel heard. We

have two ears and one mouth for a good reason. When we share a perspective, but through questions, it inspires inclusion and internal thought in another, leading them to a path that joins with us instead of against us."

"Can you explain more about that?"

"On our journey thus far, when have you had the biggest epiphanies: when you were talking, or when I asked you a question and you reflected on it?"

Jeremy paused and thought back to those moments. She's right! It was her questions that inspired thoughts within him. They motivated conversations and allowed him the space to reply and be heard by her. Asking good questions of himself can drive necessary challenges to assumptions and patterns that are followed. Asking good questions of others can inspire connection and collaboration toward common ground.

"OK, you're right," Jeremy said. "It was through good questions that so much of the lessons I've learned came to be. So, you're suggesting that I share what I've learned, but ask questions to those that I'm sharing with?"

"That's certainly an important ingredient in the process," Laluna said.

"OK, that means there's more ingredients. What are those—?"

Before Jeremy could finish his sentence, a passerby bumped into him. The passerby didn't acknowledge what he did and didn't apologize to Jeremy.

"What the heck?! What a jerk! How rude and obnoxious of him,." Jeremy said while the man sped away, still oblivious to what he had done.

"That seemed to upset you, my friend, Laluna said.

Jeremy paused to catch his breath. The lessons he learned yesterday flooded his mind again: Judgement is premature. Conclusions are premature. Labeling others can be unfair. Don't just react with the emotion that comes from within, but respond based on the positive parts of who you are inside. He felt his anger, rather, the emotion of anger, come on— anger at himself for having done what he would have done before. Was this journey for nothing? Did he learn what he thought he learned? Did he fail in his quest to learn what he thought They don't tell others? Maybe there is a They. Maybe he needs to find Them. He felt himself spinning backward. He felt his anxiety returning. Is it his anxiety, or is it just anxiety? Does he have anxiety, or, what did Laluna say? Am I experiencing anxiety? Out of desperation to stop the chaos stirring within, he turned to Laluna with all of these questions written on his face.

"It certainly can feel chaotic when we start our journey of change within," she said. "It feels chaotic for us and can instill chaos in others. We have to be patient with ourselves. We have to show compassion toward ourselves. Change certainly takes time to settle in now, doesn't it? Indeed it does, my friend. It is two steps forward and one step sideways at times. What is so wonderful about it is we can always side-step our way back to the path forward."

"But I failed. I know I'm not supposed to react that way to someone, but I did anyway."

"Oh, my friend, you are failing fast. This is all new to you. Patterns that have lived within us will persist until we persist beyond them. It is through the resilience we build that we see these missteps as challenges to overcome and learn from."

"Learn, adapt, and improve."

"Exactly my friend. Would you have caught yourself in that pattern of reaction before your journey here?"

"Oh, no way! Reactors react. That's all I knew. I wouldn't have given it another thought."

"I believe you and I believe you did more this time than you could have imagined before you arrived here. Is that so?"

"That's for sure!"

"And remember, failure is only permanent if you accept it as so. Failure is only truly a failure when we stop and deny ourselves future attempts to succeed."

"But it doesn't feel good to make these types of mistakes, now that I know better. Maybe I should wait and practice more."

"Through these trials, through testing and iterating day after day, you make progress. Life is lived when you accept progress over perfection."

"Progress over perfection?"

"Yes. There are never perfect times or perfect moments to take action. It is through action that progress is made. Accepting that will empower you forward."

"So, make progress instead of thinking things will be perfect?"

"Exactly, my friend. All this will take time. Remember, you have control over two and only two things: how you prepare to respond to your life and how you actually respond to your life. Let's talk about preparing to respond. What positive actions have you learned on your journey?"

"Well, you just mentioned one: being compassionate."

"Great! Any other positive actions you have taken on this journey when things were difficult?"

"Yeah, I would stop and take a deep breath. Sometimes I'd close my eyes."

"OK, if you were to design a response to that situation with all of that in mind, what would those steps look like?"

"Um, I guess I would stop, take a deep breath, close my eyes, and imagine that maybe that man was having a bad day, and I'd feel compassion toward him for having a bad day."

"What a wonderful way to respond to a situation!"

"Yeah, but I still reacted before I had a chance."

"But it is never too late to practice. It is a matter of mindfully intervening in those reactions to redirect our reactions to responses that we have prepared ahead of time. We rehearse. We know that things happen to us throughout our days. We prepare to respond to them and then actually respond. And when we fail to, we forgive ourselves and move forward, knowing we will have more chances. Over time, the responses become natural. We have taught what's within that how we respond is how we designed our responses."

"OK, that makes a lot of sense."

"Persistence is the key to success in this and in life. Shall we persist forward?"

As Laluna turned to resume their progress, Jeremy followed.

*Make progress over perfection,* he thought. *I can do that. Be patient and kind to yourself. That one seemed more challenging.*

In the spirit of making progress over perfection and learning the power of good questions, he turned to Laluna.

"You said to be kind to yourself," he said. "I feel like that should make sense to me, but I'm not sure I completely understand what you mean."

"Remember the compassion you showed Peruma after the disaster that happened at his party?" Laluna asked.

"Yes, I remember."

"We show compassion to others. If our friends or family struggle, we respond to them with kindness, encouragement, inspiring hope."

Well, he thought, this is a skill he hasn't had before because it isn't something that exists in his community, but he can feel this shift within him now.

"We just forget to turn that compassionate instinct toward ourselves," Laluna continued. "Don't we deserve the same kindness we give others? What we do for friends, shouldn't we do for ourselves? Shouldn't we be our best friends?"

"Our own best friends?" Jeremy asked. "How can we possibly be our own best friends? Isn't it what others think of us or need from us that matters?"

"Our puppet friends come to mind, don't they? We spend all our time with ourselves and a tremendous amount of time in conversation with ourselves. Shouldn't we be the priority?"

"But isn't that, well, selfish? Isn't helping others and adding value to others part of living your Optimal Life?"

"How do you give to another that which you do not have yourself? It is the overflowing cup that pours into another. We need to write, direct, and star in the play of our life. We pour into ourselves first. We spend time building our characters within so we show up well for others and avoid the negative patterns that so many are challenged with."

Is that what this journey has been all about, getting himself right? Was the journey to discover how to build the characters within so he can respond to life with intention, as Laluna suggested? This completely breaks away from the way Reactors live, and it certainly isn't the way Insensors live. Jeremy is already living differently within these first moments of his new life.

# IT STARTS WITH A BELIEF

Jeremy was exhausted but excited. It had been an incredible couple of days. He just wished he could make it back to his community more quickly, but he also appreciated the time to learn more and allow all the new experiences to be absorbed. He really had no idea how long it would take to get back, given they were headed in a different direction.

"I hope I can make it back before dark," Jeremy said. "I've enjoyed my time here, but I'd rather spend this coming night in my own bed and start my new life with my new knowledge in the community where I live."

Before Laluna could reply, they passed by a gated entrance of a small village, where Jeremy noticed some familiar creatures inside. There were several atometes bustling among the small crowds within the confines of the village. Each atomete followed patterns that Jeremy witnessed before. He noticed one atomete following a pattern of taking steps forward, turning away from what appeared to be nothing, and speeding away from that nothingness—only to make a less valiant attempt. Laluna and Jeremy continued to walk past the entrance, but suddenly Jeremy stopped and took a few steps backward to regain full visibility of the scene in the village.

Laluna also stopped, then asked, "Is there something wrong?"

"I don't know," Jeremy replied. "I just hate to see him struggle like that. The pneumon within the atomete keeps driving him away from making progress, and he's letting it."

"That must be frustrating for him."

"Yeah, I mean, I can imagine it would be. In fact, I know it would be because it was for me. I allowed what I thought was my anxiety to stop me from living my life. I allowed anger to drive how I showed up to others. Like you said, I can feel anger, but I don't have to act angry. I can feel an emotion and not act on that emotion. I allowed others to drive how I reacted to my life. I let others be a marionette of me. I conformed to what my community told me to conform to. I procrastinated. I didn't define what success was for my own life. I didn't even know what success could look like for me. I was a calamity in my own life, an actor in someone else's play. All the things you've told me, that's how I lived. I don't want that for him."

Jeremy motioned to the atomete in his repeated pattern of no progress. Jeremy was shocked to feel a tear in his eye as the gravity of everything he has been through bore weight down on him.

"But you broke that conformity, didn't you?" Laluna asked. "You did find a definition of success and you took action."

"Yeah, but it took me so long, and I only did it to make my mom mad. I just wanted to rebel against what she insisted I do and insisted I be."

"Would you take the best of your life right now away from yourself? Would you change it?"

"The best of my life?"

"Yes, think of the most cherished moments or the most cherished part of your life right now. Would you change it for anything?"

"No, I don't think so."

"Then you have to accept all that was, because all of what was brought the best you have now. Be careful what you wish away or what you wish to change before. You learn from your past, influence your future, but it is your moment to direct. What was simply was."

"But what will be is up to me?"

"Exactly, my friend."

Jeremy took a deep breath and wiped the tears from his eyes. He felt his chest rise. He felt his heart swell. He felt a surge of energy, a wave of peaceful energy to draw from. He looked at the village again and stepped forward. Laluna followed but kept her distance to allow him to explore on his own.

Jeremy approached the atomete that had inspired this new adventure. He stopped, not having quite thought through how he could help here, but help was his intention. He felt compassion for this being. He felt he needed to share the epiphanies he had on his journey to break the atomete free of the bondage of his patterns and the negative influence the pneumon was having on the atomete. But Jeremy continued to stand still, wondering how to achieve this next milestone of success he felt he was moving toward.

Then doubt entered Jeremy's mind. Who was he to help anyone? He barely knew how to help himself. He was barely a newborn into this life. Who was he to impose his new discoveries on another? Maybe he was being foolish to think he could really change. Reactors react. Maybe that was his destiny, to be a Reactor, or maybe even a...

He paused. He couldn't bring himself to say it. Having the thought staggered him back a few steps, and having accepted those backward steps caused him to turn away from the atomete.

"Maybe I'll try again another time or maybe later," Jeremy said loud enough for Laluna to hear, but he avoided eye contact with her.

"It starts with a belief,." Laluna said.

"What? What starts with a belief?" Jeremy asked.

"Everything worth doing."

"I don't understand. A belief in what?"

"A belief in yourself. A belief in your ability to take action. A belief that you can withstand adversity, disappointment, failure, falling short, mistakes, and even success itself."

"Well, clearly I don't have a belief in any of it." Jeremy said while, looking back at the atomete he abandoned.

"What would you say to your best friend?"

The immediacy of that lesson came flooding back to him, and he felt defiance surge into him.

"I don't have a best friend," Jeremy said.

"OK. What would you say to me if I said that to you?" Laluna asked.

The words from Laluna stormed over him as few have in the past. She was a friend. She was a true friend. Look at what she's done for him? Look at all they've been through on this journey? Jeremy has known Laluna for only two days, but he felt closer to her than anyone else in his life. Was she his best friend? Was this what true friendship looked like?

"I would, well, I guess, encourage you," Jeremy replied. "I would tell you to be patient with yourself. I'd tell you to show compassion to yourself. I'd remind you that change takes time, but taking action will help you to instill more of the lessons for yourself."

These words flowing from Jeremy was an unexpected torrent that surprised Laluna as much him.

"My friend, that was beautiful! Do you think you can express this to yourself? Is there a question here that you can ask yourself that might help?"

Ah yes, the questions. He nearly forgot to ask himself good questions.

"Will this bring me closer or further away from my success? And my success is an Optimal Life. So, the action of helping the atomete, will this bring me closer or further away from living my Optimal Life? I get it now! Of course it will! And what do I have to worry about? Failure? Failure is only momentary. Failure is my opportunity to learn. If I deny the atomete my action and I deny myself the opportunity to take action, then I deny both of us the opportunity to grow."

With all of this released into the afternoon air, Jeremy turned back from where he retreated, but this time with intention and focus. He didn't know exactly what he was going to do, but that was OK. He knew his intentions were good, and he felt that he could embrace the idea of being emotionally and intellectually agile.

"An action taken with intent is an action worth taking," Laluna said. "You are preparing to respond to your life and actually respond in a way that's aligned to your purposeful meaning, the intended value of your life."

Jeremy approached the atomete, who continued his pattern, back and forth.

"Um, excuse me," Jeremy said to the atomete. "I think I can help you. See, you don't have to just do what the pneumon within you says to do. You just have to get in tune with it. You..." The atomete bustled past Jeremy. Clearly, Jeremy's words didn't reach him.

Jeremy took a slight step back and looked to the ground in hopes of calling on his will to prevent him from turning away again. As the atomete repeated his pattern, passing Jeremy again, Jeremy had a second chance to reach him.

"Just stop!" Jeremy ordered. "Stand in one place, and close your eyes! You can find peace, even in chaos!"

Jeremy hoped his raised voice and urgent expression would break through this time. But the atomete continued on.

Jeremy threw a desperate look at Laluna. He felt the urge to leave the scene. He felt embarrassment set in. Is everyone staring at him? What if they think he's a fool?

Laluna stepped forward. "We think about ourselves most of the time, so we think others do as well, as if their attention is always pointing toward us," she said. "It rarely is as much as we'd like to think."

"This isn't working," Jeremy said. "He isn't listening to me."

"Sometimes we aren't ready to hear. Do you recall feeling encouraged along your journey?"

"Yes, several times."

"What seemed to encourage you along your way?"

Jeremy paused to think. What did encourage him? It seemed like just having Laluna by his side encouraged him. What was it about her? He was always such a rebel. What made him not rebel against her attempts? His mother came to mind. She was always so aggressive toward him. She preached at him and never talked with him. He never felt she was just...wait, that's it!

"I think just having someone by my side was encouraging," Jeremy said. "You helped, but didn't push. You guided me but didn't always direct me."

Jeremy turned his attention to the atomete again. He approached the atomete and matched the atomete's stride side-by-side. When the pneumon welled up with energy inside the atomete, Jeremy simply put his hand on the atomete's shoulder and remained calm.

"It's OK, my friend. It's OK to feel scared," Jeremy said to the atomete in a calm, reassuring voice.

For the first time, the atomete paused, gasped, and allowed the air to release slowly. The pneumon became more insistent, and the atomete gave in and turned away again. But Jeremy stayed with him and kept talking.

"I know how you feel," he said. "I've been there. It isn't easy to not let what's within us drive our reactions. I used to be a Reactor, or at least that's what they told me I was. But I'm not one after all! Maybe we can try again, or rather, let's do our best together and see what happens."

The atomete looked at Jeremy for the first time with pleading eyes as he wanted to say, "I want to."

Jeremy and the atomete turned around and walked toward the point of the atomete's typical return. The pneumon inside the atomete became frantic and energized. The atomete slowed, but Jeremy continued to encourage him.

"It's OK," Jeremy said. "Let's only do what you can, but maybe a little more than you think you can. See, if you lean into these moments, the pneumon inside you will learn that you are strong and can live these moments without turning away. Can you do that? I'm right here."

The atomete paused, started to take a step back, but changed the direction of that step to one, then two, then three steps forward. Instead of turning away, the atomete stood still. He took a small step backward and looked at Jeremy.

"It's OK, my friend," Jeremy said. "Just take your time."

The pneumon kept flailing about within the atomete with ever-increasing energy. Jeremy again put his hand on the atomete's shoulder to reassure him. The atomete stepped back again, but shook his head, closed his eyes, and took a deep breath in and out. He took two, then three steps forward. The pneumon began to increase its intensity, but after the atomete took another step forward with another deep breath in and out, the pneumon began to settle down. Jeremy couldn't believe his eyes.

With his hand on the atomete's shoulder, Jeremy could feel the atomete relax. The atomete looked at the pneumon and smiled to acknowledge the pneumon's efforts. The atomete took another deep breath and three more steps forward. Jeremy stayed by his side for those additional steps. The atomete paused and looked at Jeremy with a tear in his eye and an expression of joy and gratitude, and then he began to take full strides forward on his path.

Jeremy watched his new friend make his way without hindrance. An incredible sense of accomplishment swept through Jeremy. He had never felt like this. For him to help someone break out of a pattern they were in was incredible. He wanted to do more, see more of these changes. It was as if he had a superpower that he could now use for the betterment of others.

"Many more opportunities to have moments like these will come your way, my friend," Laluna said as she joined Jeremy.

"That felt amazing," Jeremy said. "I actually helped him, truly helped him!"

Jeremy paused while his mind continued to process the excitement of his new experience.

"This truly does feel like the way to live an Optimal Life," he said a few minutes later. "Living your life with intention and adding value to others."

"Indeed! You have come a very long way from the limited thinking you brought here to the expanded way of thinking you now possess," Laluna said. "That expansion can continue as you embrace the lessons and look for opportunities to stretch yourself just beyond the limits you might think you have."

"Beyond the limits I think I have? What do you mean?"

"We so often impose limits on ourselves that aren't truly limits. We accept the limits others have of themselves when they project them onto us. We internalize them. Others believe they can't, so they insist you can't, either. They don't believe in themselves, so they insist you don't, either."

"Why is that?"

"Fear! What would it say about them if you proved you could? It would force them to question where they are in their own lives and where they are not. They might not be ready to do so. So often, we passively accept those limitations without challenging them. You don't know what your limits are until you press up against them, feel the resistance, and then push through them."

"What kind of resistance are you talking about?"

Laluna stopped and bent to pick up a small twig on the ground. She held it out so that Jeremy could take it.

"If I suggested to you that by picking up this twig and moving it up and down, you would build strong muscles, would you believe me?" Laluna asked.

"No way! It's too light," Jeremy replied. "I'd never build my muscles by lifting it."

"Indeed you wouldn't. It provides very little, if any, resistance for your muscles. We need to push ourselves, push through healthy resistance in order to achieve the growth we need in our lives. Why not pick that up?" Laluna asked as she motioned to a very large rock on the ground just off the path.

"That's way too heavy. I'd probably hurt myself trying to pick it up."

"It is a matter of finding balance, my friend. We want to stretch beyond what we think our limits are, but do so mindfully, ensuring we take care of ourselves through the process."

They continued walking down the path as Jeremy reflected on what just happened. What Laluna was saying became clearer and clearer to him. His entire community convinced him that he was a Reactor, that he would be nothing more than either a Reactor or an Insensor. They convinced him that he would never and could never be more than everyone else was, but all of it was just their own limitations projected onto him. He just wished he had realized this sooner. Why did he allow them to do that to him? Why didn't he break free earlier?

The image of the reggrats came to mind. He remembered the lockers opening, shooting those books at them, and closing. Is recalling what he's recalling right now serving him? Is it helping him? The answer was clear to Jeremy. He needed to start leaving the past where it belongs.

*What was simply was but what will be is up to me.*

# TAKING THE LAST STEPS

Laluna and Jeremy rounded another corner on the path toward Jeremy's community. They hadn't traveled for very long, and Jeremy wasn't sure how long it would take to get back. This was a new path and a new journey he was on.

He heard some familiar noises just beyond the bushes nearby. He headed over to see what was provoking his memory and was astonished to find he was back at the labyrinth that was near to the start of his journey! Jeremy's head whipped around to find Laluna just behind him.

"How did we get back to this point so quickly?" Jeremy asked. "Is this the same labyrinth we passed before?"

"Why yes it is, my friend," Laluna said. "The journey takes what you need it to take and brings you to where you need to be. You just have to take the actions to bring you as far as you have come."

"I can't believe it! We are nearly there. I should head straight back now. I could be there in a matter of minutes."

Jeremy turned to leave, but glanced back at the creatures in the labyrinth. They faced the same challenges as before. So many were struggling, incessantly talking without action, and some were still going in every direction except toward the exit.

Jeremy paused to think through his next steps. *What if I could help them? What if I could make a difference here?*

He looked around and spotted something he hadn't noticed on his first visit—an arched bridge strategically placed in the corner of the clearing. The bridge was the same size as the labyrinth and could stretch from the labyrinth's entrance to its exit. Why hadn't anyone noticed the bridge before? Well, the creatures were certainly too small to put it in place, but Jeremy wasn't. What a perfect opportunity to help the creatures achieve the success they seek.

Jeremy walked to the bridge, picked it up, and placed it over the labyrinth, creating an easy passage over the maze below. He stepped back, rubbed his hands together triumphantly, and smiled to wait for the amazing results.

Slowly, each creature noticed the bridge. Some looked at the others first. Some headed straight for it, but eventually, most began to cross the bridge over the labyrinth. They were easily making their way toward the finish line.

Jeremy looked at Laluna with a smile. "Well, that was easy, so it isn't their journey now," he said. "Isn't that great!?"

"I wonder without problems, without challenge, without resistance, what one learns," Laluna said. "I wonder how one prepares without anything to prepare against."

"What do you mean?" Jeremy asked, looking back at his masterpiece. But the answer revealed itself as soon as he asked the question. When the creatures exited the labyrinth, they spun in circles. Some entered the labyrinth at the exit and wandered toward the starting point. Other creatures fought, quibbled, and sought conflict with others. It was complete, utter chaos.

"I don't understand what happened," Jeremy said. "I wanted to help them like you helped me. I found my way to my success on this journey because you helped me along my way. I wanted to do the same for them, as you said, help and add value to others."

"Was this an easy journey for you, my friend?" Laluna asked.

"No way! It was... OK, I get it! You're saying it was the challenge of the journey itself that allowed me to achieve the success I did. You're saying that these creatures need to take their own journeys and face their own challenges, so once they cross their finish lines, they are prepared to do so."

"You have learned so much! We want to add value to others, but they have to find their own way. We live by example, and we can be that example to others. We can guide others, empower others, but it is their choice, their decisions, and the actions they take that will build who they become.

Jeremy turned the bridge around, leading the creatures back to the beginning. Once all were off, he removed the bridge for good. The creatures resumed their respective struggles to make it through the labyrinth to their own successes.

"I think, no, I know I'm ready to head back home now." Jeremy said to Laluna, turning back to the path he originally came down.

"Let's go!"

But Laluna stayed where she stood. Jeremy turned back after a few steps with the obvious question written all over his face.

"I agree," Laluna said. "You are ready to take that next step, and I think it is an important one to take on your own. You have come so far. The next triumph is yours to enjoy and experience."

"But I'll miss you. I mean, I have just really enjoyed traveling with you and, well, you've become my friend. I think you're the first friend I've ever had."

"And we will continue to be friends. I have cherished my time with you, and I'm so grateful you accepted my company."

"Oh, that's it! I'm grateful! I have, um, gratitude for you. I mean, I want to show you gratitude for what you've done for me. Yesterday seems like a lifetime ago, and the moment I was stuck, it was you that helped to ensure I took my first step and so many more along my way. I don't think I would have learned what I've learned or found out what living an Optimal Life was all about without you."

"That means a lot, it really does. I genuinely appreciate that. I will be here if you ever decide to come back. The future is untold. What is ahead for you and what is ahead for me is undetermined, but with our determination, the possibilities are endless."

"I like the sound of that. I don't know if I'll come back. I'd like to think I'll visit, but how will I find you?"

"When the wall's opening appears, I'll know to come. I've always come no matter who chooses to change their life."

"You have helped the others, haven't you?"

"Indeed, I have and others have as well. We live our Optimal Life much the same as you've discovered it to be. We here in this community look to add value and help others as we can, no more and never less."

"I don't need to know how far they went or what they learned. I would have wanted to know before, but it doesn't seem to matter now. They took the journey that they could, I imagine. I do hope to meet them, and maybe we can learn from one another."

"What a wonderful thought to have, my friend. What a wonderful opportunity awaits you."

He thought back to the moment that his community's wall seemed impenetrable, but it was the energy that came with his decision to leave that created the undisclosed opening.

Jeremy felt confident that Laluna would keep her word and return upon his return. He glanced over his shoulder toward the path he would take home and turned back to Laluna for a final goodbye.

"OK, then that settles it," Jeremy said. "I will finish this journey on my own, and will return to visit when I can. This has been more than I could have imagined. Thank you again, my friend Laluna."

"You are so welcome, my friend Jeremy. Until we come together again."

# A LITTLE SURRENDERING

Jeremy made his way down the path, back toward the community he had left just the day before. He was at a near run, driven by the anticipation of seeing his community and all the people he knows through his new perspective. There was a huge shift inside of him. He couldn't wait to tell the Reactors that they don't have to be Reactors, that they can be anything they want. He hoped that the Insensors would hear his words. He hoped it wasn't too late for them. He wanted more for them, all of them. Yes, even his mother. He couldn't believe he was thinking these thoughts, but why can't his mother be more than she is? He did it!

As he continued his walk, the wall of his community came into sight. As he gained ground toward it, he had a nervous thought. The passage appeared for him but closed behind him. Would it appear for him again? How would he get back in? He felt his emotions spiral toward negative thoughts.

*Remember the lesson,* he thought. *Anticipating the bad brings the bad that much closer to becoming real. Imagining negative outcomes brings their potential closer to becoming realized. The future isn't determined. I only have my moment, and right now, my moment says I keep going and trust I will be emotionally and intellectually agile enough for what's to come.*

Jeremy was nearly there. As the wall became

clearer in his vision, he noticed something that surprised him even after all he had seen. There was an open entrance in plain sight, right in front of the path he was on. What was previously closed was wide open and waiting. Relief swept over him with this knowledge that he could finally experience his community with a perspective that was new to him and foreign to them.

He felt a moment's apprehension from the gravity of that thought. He imagined how he would be perceived and received by others. But he quickly reminded himself of Laluna's lesson. He would show up as he should, and how others respond is a commentary on them, not him. He would show up authentically, with clarity on his inner standard and respond to others aligned with that standard. He will prepare to respond and actually respond by his design. If he fell short in his moment, he would forgive himself and move forward positively.

That thought carried him through the threshold, and as he passed, the entrance behind him closed. Briefly, he was concerned about that happening, but this thought was drowned out by the enormity of his current experience as he looked at his community for the first time since he left.

Gone was the color. Gone was the vibrance. Gone was the diversity of experience. All that was left was what he left behind for that short time—a colorless, drab environment with Reactors and Insensors. He stood there for what felt like an eternity. His eyes scanned, then darted from spot to spot desperately while he looked for a place to start his mission.

He had discovered that there wasn't a Them or a

They. Instead, his experiences throughout the journey gave him the insights, or rather the ingredients, that would lead to living an Optimal Life. It wasn't something relegated to mythology. It was real! It was possible! Who would he tell first? Who would hear him? As this moment extended, his immediate hope declined. He knew nothing would change without action, so he decided to get off the dead-center where he stood and make his first attempt.

"Excuse me. Excuse me. See, you think you're a Reactor, but you don't really have to be. See, I went on this…" Jeremy said to the first person he saw, but they continued on as if they never heard him..

"You don't have to carry this around. It is the weight of your past that isn't helping…," Jeremy said to an Insensor lumbering by while pointing at their bag of rocks. Again, the Insensor continued walking without even a glance of acknowledgement.

Jeremy paused and remembered the atomete. It was the moment Jeremy met the atomete where he was and walked by his side with encouragement that the atomete took notice. Jeremy approached someone else showing the clear actions of a Reactor and walked next to her.

"It seems like you are frustrated. Is there anything I can do to help?" Jeremy said to her.

With a furrowed brow of confusion from the Reactor and a slight glance toward Jeremy, Jeremy felt those two sentences might have been heard, although it was a transient moment at best.

Jeremy decided to push on and draw on his experience with the atomete to see if he could reach her.

When he was closer to the Reactor, he extended

his hand and placed it on her shoulder as an attempt at reassurance and connection and said, "You can live a better…"

"Take your hand away from me boy!" the Reactor snapped. "Who the hell do you think you are? God! You young people, always running your mouths!" She shrugged Jeremy's hand off of her shoulder and quickened her pace.

Jeremy stopped and looked at the ground with dismay. Why aren't his attempts working? They worked out there, why not here? He sought change, why won't they? What was the difference? Noggy? Was it that foul substance sedating others from seeing the potential to change? The lesson of judging came to mind. Is he judging others unfairly? Is this about expectations? Is this about controlling others?

*No, I mean, maybe,* he thought. *I don't want to control them. I just want to help them. But maybe it's about living my own life and others living theirs. How do I get them to change then?* Ugh! He wished he could ask Laluna or hear her guidance about this.

Would his parents react the same way? He was both apprehensive and excited to see his home and parents from his new perspective. The anticipation of what's to come seems to fall short of the reality once realized. His lessons of anxiety showed him that. What is to come is built in his mind first and so often overdone. Jeremy decided to just focus on his walk home and continued reflection of the lessons he had gained in the last two days.

Living an Optimal Life isn't a destination, but a process. He had to be patient with himself and others. The patterns that he followed for all of his life would not simply disappear because he knew better. What was inside would still drive momentary reactions that might not align to who he knows himself to be. With time, who he wants to be and who he is to others will be in harmony. Mistakes will be made, of course, but, as Laluna said, he has control over two and only two things in his life: how he prepares to respond and how he actually responds. He knew this would be hard work.

He knew it would take time and patience, but as he made his way home and looked around his community, he couldn't find a single source of support. Would he have to bear this weight alone? Would he face each challenge with no one to turn to? All of this raced through his mind as he looked up and realized he had arrived home.

His excitement had waned a bit, likely quickened by emotional and physical fatigue that had set in. It had been an incredible but exhausting two days. He had seen so much, learned so much, experienced more in that time than all previous times combined. He felt apprehension set in as he approached the door. Did he have the strength within to encounter his mother right now? What would he say? Would she yell? Well, that was likely, given her pattern would be same as a Reactor. How would he react, or rather, respond? "Prepare to respond and actually respond.

There's a difference between living in the future through anxiety, anticipating events that might not even happen, and otherwise preparing for life to occur. As Laluna said, Living in the wreckage of our future denies us the joy of our moments."

That lesson stood out in Jeremy's mind at this moment. The idea of being intellectually and emotionally agile also came to mind. He realized that he only has so much energy within him to respond well to his life. What's within him was telling him that it was time to rest.

With these thoughts coming together, he reached for the doorknob, turned it, and opened the door slowly.

"Where the hell have you been?" his mother bellowed. "Screwing off again, I bet! Once a loser, always a loser. Once a failure, always a…"

His mother's words were interrupted by something that shocked both her and Jeremy.

Without hesitation, Jeremy quietly embraced his mother by wrapping his arms around her and gently squeezing her.

"I love you mom," Jeremy said.

His mother froze, stiff with shock, denying her reaction to Jeremy's affection. Jeremy didn't care that she might not change. He didn't care how she reacted to him. He decided to live with compassion toward others and express love, regardless of whether that love was returned. This would be part of his mental core, the essence of who he is and what drives how he shows up in his life.

He released her, gently smiled, turned, and walked up the stairs to his room.

His mother broke the silence just before Jeremy reached the top of the stairs.

"What the hell was that? I mean, I don't understand. I mean, why did you…"

Jeremy drowned his mother's confusion by closing the bedroom door behind him. Silence. The sound of silence deafened his ears at first, but what followed was a wave of peace. It was time for him to recharge. To live quietly within the moment he had in the confines of his space. He walked a few steps and fell face first on his bed. He wanted to dream of what was and what will be for him. He wondered what would come in his sleep and what would come with tomorrow. And, with those thoughts, sleep came to meet him.

## EMPOWERING OTHERS

Jeremy had never slept so deeply and soundly as he did that night. It felt like only a moment had passed from the time he fell asleep until the morning began. He felt the energy return from the night before. He was ready to take on the day. He had a new focus and began to think of what his next steps would be. What did success truly look like for him? Living an Optimal Life looks different for different people, so what did it look like for him? He thought about how he spent his time before his journey began—day in and day out, just reacting to his life situations without any purpose.

He thought about that word, *intention*. He wasn't living with intention. He likely would have never realized that if he hadn't stopped drinking noggy. Taking that rebellious step pried his eyes open wide enough to see more than he had seen before, more opportunities than seemed possible. But it was the action he took that showed him what was possible, that instilled motivation to take more steps, building momentum throughout his journey. Action first, then motivation, as Laluna would say. We are the cavalry!

He did so much, but there was so much more to do in his life. Was it school? Was it helping to change his community? Was it to travel again beyond these walls? What was to be was up to him. He also remembered that patience was crucial for success. None of this would happen instantaneously. It will be through taking consistent steps forward through inspired action that will carve the life out the way he was meant to live. And, with that thought in mind, he sprang from bed, ready to take his first steps of the first day following the last.

He entered the hall to find the familiar scene: his mother rushing about and his father lumbering aimlessly.

"Oh, nice of you to get up," his mother bellowed. "It's about time! You're going to make us late, and you're making me mad!"

Even though they traveled separately, she still insisted that somehow Jeremy made her late if he was late. It was just another of his mother's attempts at causing unnecessary conflict.

"Good morning, Mom. How's it going today?" Jeremy asked.

She stopped for a moment, stunned by Jeremy's question.

"How's it going? What the hell has gotten into you? It's going terribly because we're going to be late, and you're acting weird. Now, knock it off!"

Jeremy walked over to his mother, put his hand on her shoulder, and said, "It's OK, Mom. I'm sorry you're frustrated. I'll hurry, and we can leave and not be late."

Jeremy's response to his mother caught what little attention his father had. He looked at Jeremy and lifted his hand as if he wanted a moment of contact.

"You need to knock it off," Jeremy's mother said in a slightly less intense tone. "I don't know what's going on with you.".

Jeremy walked over to his dad and smiled.

"Hey, Dad. I have so much to tell you when you're ready to hear it. Things can be better. You can be better."

His dad lifted his head in an attempt to straighten his back a little and tried to smile. The corners of his mouth managed to curve upward slightly.

"Let's GO!" his Mother yelled. Her voice shattered the beginnings of a tender moment into tiny pieces.

"Oh, and you can find your noggy ready and waiting in the kitchen," she continued in a snide tone.

Jeremy felt anxiety and anger rush into his body simultaneously. He whipped his head around to meet anger with anger. He locked eyes with his mother, who was smirking at him. Her expression showed a moment of triumph, where she believed she could cause Jeremy to return to the son she believed he was.

As the anger welled inside of him, he began to work through it and found the strength to stop. He physically and emotionally took a step back from the moment. He looked down to collect his thoughts and look at what's within to find the next action to take. He found compassion.

That was the key to it: *How she lives is how she lives. It doesn't have to impose itself on me,* Jeremy thought. *This is my life, not hers. How I show up in my life is mine to determine.*

"I won't be drinking the noggy, Mom, but thanks. I'm sorry if that upsets you. Let's get going so we aren't late."

With that, Jeremy turned away to quickly finish getting ready for his day. He left his mother in an uncharacteristic silence, her mouth agape.

As good as that felt, Jeremy also felt the energy that this experience took from him. He wondered what the day would bring—whether it would be the same as before but without his normal Reactor reactions to go along with it.

He reminded himself that to anticipate the future with worry doesn't help. But what about school? What was the point of going there? He learned nothing while he was acting as a Reactor. He imagined learning less, now that his vision was clearer.

How would he help those in this community? He can't control others. He can't make them listen. He can't...well, wait. There was the book! The book that started it all. The fragments within that inspired his journey. Those must have been the attempts to share what others had learned. The fragments reflected what others had learned and were able to recall upon their return.

Jeremy ventured farther than the others and discovered more than them, so he could share more. Was that it? Was that how he could provide value and positively impact others?

Suddenly, the school was exactly where he needed to be. He sped through his routine of getting ready.

"Bye, Mom!" Jeremy yelled as he rushed out the door and to his bike. He stopped thinking about his mother's need to leave at the same time, which caused conflict between them. That was her challenge to work through, not his.

The ride to class reminded him of the difficulty his community posed. He passed, yet again, the sign with those words that resonated with him before, but were absurd to him now: "What was will always be."

*How do they accept this way of living?* Jeremy thought

while he watched the people in his community through his new perspective on living. He remembered Laluna's words, "You can't resolve what you won't allow."

If the people in his community only rely on noggy to minimize their own state of living and never take steps to actually resolve the challenges within, then nothing changes.

Nothing changes unless willfully changed. Do they have the will to change? Do any of them have the will to do what Jeremy is in the process of doing? He listened to his mom spew negativity into the world. He thought of the atometes and how whatever they said went right into their pneumons. He also remembered that what others said went into the pneumons inside the atometes as well.

Was this happening here? Was all the negative his mom and any other Reactor speaking around him and to him building up within him? He felt a moment of panic. How could he stop that from happening? Does he know how to do that? Is it even possible?

He arrived at school, jumped off his bike, and quickly locked it. His excitement returned. He wanted to pour his thoughts out on those pages. He wanted to share all of it with anyone willing to read it. But who would?

*I guess that's not within my control,* Jeremy thought. *All I can do is add value. What's done with it is what's done with it.*

Being aware of the impact that others had on him, Jeremy wanted to go to the library quickly to avoid interacting with others. He wanted to ensure what he learned wouldn't be tainted before he could release it. He felt he was in a race to convey all the lessons he learned before they slipped away under the weight of the barrages from others.

Jeremy rushed through the halls, toward the library. He intentionally avoided listening to what the Reactor students were saying and seeing them act out. He flung himself into the library, as if he had just crossed the finish line of a marathon. He couldn't wait to get to the book, to look at what was there with knowing eyes. But, of course, it was still behind locked doors, and interacting with Ms. Goldston, the gatekeeper of the key, would bring more exposure to what he wanted to avoid.

He took a deep breath and remembered that others aren't allowed to dictate how he feels within. What's within is for him to influence and direct, not others.

*Mindful exposure to the negative can strengthen me,* he thought. *I can only grow through resistance, so it is a matter of balancing being around the negative at times and seeking the positive.*

He made his way to the desk where Ms. Goldston sat, head down and busy.

"Excuse me," Jeremy said. "I was hoping…"

"Oh, I bet you were! Let me guess. You want the key to get at that damn book. You're all the same. You come back here, confused and desperate, thinking you were going to find something that you failed to find. Once a failure, always a failure." Jeremy felt the sting in Ms. Goldston's words while she reached in the drawer and tossed the keys in his direction without even looking up at him.

He started to explain that he wasn't the others. He wanted her to know how far he went and how far he had come. He wanted her to see who he had become, but he quickly closed his mouth, followed by his eyes. He took a deep breath. Changing others isn't done through attacking as the initial urge would have him do. Change comes from living the change. Explaining himself to others doesn't mean they will hear him. They have to be ready and willing to receive, and Ms. Goldston showed no signs of that readiness.

"Thank you for the keys," Jeremy said. "I appreciate it. I can imagine this isn't an easy job. Maybe you can tell me about it sometime."

Jeremy's response surprised him.

Ms. Goldston slowly lifted her head and tilted it to one side. With a slightly confused look on her face, she stared at Jeremy as if she were trying to understand the source of the words she just heard. She looked down briefly and then back at Jeremy. He saw the corner of her mouth move ever so slightly toward her ears, and her eyes began to water. She quickly wiped away all evidence of her facial gesture and looked down to focus on her work.

"Just go about the fool's errand you are on with that book of myths and insanity and leave me to my work," she said.

"No problem. Thank you again."

Jeremy's reply surprised him again, as well as Ms. Goldston. She looked up briefly as Jeremy turned. Apparently she hadn't encountered responses like Jeremy's from anyone else she interacted with.

The concepts of preparing to respond and actually responding was going through Jeremy's mind. He had decided how to respond ahead of time. He was able to keep his reactions to himself. The more he would do this, the more it would just be how he naturally responded. He could see that now.

Jeremy made his way to the mythology section. It struck him how absurd it was for this incredible book of potential to reside there. But it spoke to the pervasive challenges in his community. Everyone here sees living as They live, living a better life to be a myth.

Laluna said that "everything starts with a belief. If you don't believe something is possible, then you have denied the possibility for yourself." It took a belief in himself that he was meant for something more for him to ignore where the book lived and look to it for the possibilities it held for him.

Jeremy's hands shook while he fumbled with the keys. He felt all the lessons bottled up inside. Without anyone to hear him, it was up to the book to receive them. He managed to open the door and make his way to the book's resting place.

He started flipping through the mostly empty pages to find the few phrases that initially inspired his journey: "be compassionate," "Find Purposeful Meaning," and "They live an Optimal Life." None of these phrase made sense to him before, but now, he could finally fill in the gaps.

He reached into his bag and pulled out his pen, ready to write, but as he put the pen to the page, he hesitated. He had so much to say, so what was the source of his hesitation? His thoughts went to the creatures in the labyrinth. He was so sure that by solving their problems, he would help them achieve success, but it only caused chaos. He learned that each creature needed to find their way, choose their path.

The tree told Jeremy that all paths lead to where

he can be. If he wrote all he knew here, would the potential reader simply accept that as the answer? Would they find their own path? That's what's important, right? Leaving! Taking the step. Making the decision to leave, which opens the doorway out of the community and into the unknown. That is where it all began for Jeremy: stepping from the known to the unknown and continually making the decision to take the next step, the next action. It was the exposure to the experiences that made him see things differently. It was all he witnessed and the conversations along the way that led him to understand what an Optimal Life could be.

Would pouring everything he knows into this book empower the next person in the same way? It was the fragments that inspired him. That's all the previous adventurers could tell another. They might not have truly understood what they were writing. Who knows how far they got? It wasn't until those final moments before turning around to head back that it all started to come together.

Was that why so little was here for him to see initially? What could he add that would do more but not too much? What would have helped him?

With pen in hand, he pressed against the final page in the book and wrote, "Living better is not a myth. There is more for you. Take your journey. Don't stop until you know what these words truly mean. You will know when it's time. You will find Them along your way. Push past the limits you believe you have. Lean into the experiences. You can be more. You can do more. I believe in you! You've got this! Now, GO!"

He closed the book, knowing that would be the

last time he would read it. As he walked away from the book on the pedestal toward the reference desk, he heard arguing. It was Ms. Goldston and a woman who was close to Jeremy's age. He was struck by her beauty. She seemed different from the rest of the people in his community. Not quite what he witnessed beyond these walls, but, still, different.

"Oh, another one of you absurd young people," Ms. Goldston said. "Let me guess. You want the keys to the book."

"I'm not the absurd one," the woman said. "You are! I'm going to find out—"

"What They don't tell others?" Jeremy asked the woman. He handed the keys to her.

"Don't skip any parts, but the ending is the best." Jeremy said.

He smiled as the woman grabbed the keys. With a scoff, the woman strolled to the door and unlocked it. She walked into the mythology section, the same section that Jeremy had just left for good.

# ASSOCIATIONS AND HARMONY

Jeremy opened his eyes to the morning light. Several weeks had passed since his return. He laid in bed for a moment to feel the sensations of his body and observe the thoughts going through his head. It seemed that the noise from within had become louder since his return. It was as if the echoes of those around him were reverberating back through him. He closed his eyes to look inward and push them away. He wanted to remember what Laluna said, something about not controlling, not suppressing what comes from within. But, what then? Argh, what was that lesson?

*Oh, never mind,* he thought. He jumped out of bed and sprinted into the hall. He saw his mother rushing down the stairs. If her back wasn't hunched, she could move faster.

*What a ridiculous woman she is,* Jeremy thought. That thought entered his mind and left his mouth before he thought about intervening.

Why didn't that thought sit right with him? He had it countless times before, but isn't that judgment? Isn't judgment—what did Laluna say—premature?

Jeremy shook his head as if to rid himself of the confusion. Then his father lumbered by.

"Hey, old man," Jeremy said in a snide tone.

Again, a sensation rose within Jeremy. It seemed

like a cousin to the anxiety he hoped would leave him after his return to the community. He sensed that his actions were not what he wanted, but his actions seemed to be driven on his behalf. Was he losing his intention?

He came into the kitchen, only to see a glass of noggy waiting for him on the table. His anger flared inside, and he desperately wanted to throw that awful drink at his mother.

The fairies immediately came to mind. Jeremy remembered that fellow sitting there without a care as the fairies buzzed about, working so hard to evoke a reaction from him.

Jeremy took a deep breath, looked at his mother, and said. "Thank you, but no thank you. I'm heading to work."

Jeremy quit school to focus on saving more money. He had almost reached his goal, allowing him to move out on his own. The job was a stretch for him, but the hiring manager said he hadn't met anyone like Jeremy before and gave him the job regardless of his lack of experience. He loved the extra cash, but he didn't love how being there made him feel. The stress was intense as he tried desperately to convince himself and others he knew what he was doing. He was smart enough to make it somewhat convincing, but not enough to make him comfortable with it.

In fact, feeling comfortable seemed to be in short supply. No matter where he was, no matter whom he interacted with, it was always there. A gnawing feeling within him ate away at his will. Why does it always seem to be there? It is like an ever-present sensation telling him something is wrong. But what is it that's wrong?

He thought back to his journey. Was there something he had learned along the way that would help him understand what was happening and what to do? He was feeling more isolated. There was no one here he could talk to. No one would understand or even hear him. He needed a friend. He needed his best friend, Laluna.

No one creates success on their own. He remembered those words. He had taken so many steps forward. Maybe this was him taking those steps sideways. Maybe he needed to sidestep his way back onto his path toward success, but how? There didn't seem to be hope in doing so here. The longer he stayed here, the more distant the journey became, and the farther away the mountain's shadow seemed.

If not here, then, maybe, just maybe, it had to be there! Maybe he needed to find his friend, Laluna, and seek her guidance once again. But this is where he lived. This is his community. He was born among the Reactors and the Insensors. Who was he to say it wasn't enough? Wasn't it part of his defined success to change his community? But is that his job?

He was more desperate to find answers. This wasn't good for him. He knew that much. He could feel the terrible sensations within him return and grow stronger and stronger day by day. It was time to seek help. It was time for him to leave once again and find Laluna.

Jeremy left his house with intention. He was excited to see his friend again and equally excited to seek her wisdom and guidance. He felt little apprehension. There was none of the normal feelings, hesitation, or doubt. He even felt the stress within him take a step back from its attack on his insides. This release doubled his pace toward the community's wall.

As he approached, he stopped, surprised at what he saw in front of him. Instead of a small doorway, an entire archway appeared, ready and waiting to accept him. He looked around to see if anyone noticed, but as he expected, no one did. Every Reactor and Insensor simply walked on by. He smiled and continued to walk right through the giant entrance to where he wanted to be and exited from where he had always been.

The vibrance around him came into sight. The smells, the sounds—all that he enjoyed from before was there for him to behold once again. He felt the sensations that plagued him subside. He felt excitement for life's return.

He remembered Laluna saying that she would know when the wall's opening appeared. He looked around, hoping she would simply be there, but she wasn't. Not to be deterred for even a moment, he started down the path he had traveled once before, but it felt different. He had arrived there months before with so much fear and apprehension. It now felt as if he had come home in a way. Was that it? Had what was within shifted so much from his experience that what was previously his home was no longer? As those thoughts flooded into him, he heard a welcomed, familiar sound.

"Why hello, my friend! So wonderful to see you back here."

He turned to the adjacent path to find Laluna walking toward him with a warm and welcoming smile.

"Laluna, I came back because I'm confused," Jeremy said. "See, I went back to write in the book and realized maybe I shouldn't write everything in there. You said people need to find their own path. There was this woman talking to the librarian, so I gave her the keys to the room so she could read the book, but my mother was still being horrible to me, and no one wanted to be helped. But you warned me about that. I got a job, but I don't feel qualified to be there, so I keep feeling horrible inside. And that horrible feeling keeps coming back, and maybe I shouldn't be there anymore. And…"

Laluna put her hand on his shoulder and gazed into his eyes. Jeremy could see from her expression that she cared about what he was going through.

"My friend, it is good to see you here," Laluna said. "You have experienced a lot since you returned to your community. I hear you and I'm here with you. You are not alone. Why don't we walk for a while and enjoy each other's company?"

Jeremy sighed heavily into the cool air. He felt a release come from within. The urgency left him. A sense of peace returned. The lessons of "things take time," and "be patient and kind with yourself" came to mind. He turned to walk side by side with his companion, his friend.

"Laluna, how have you been?" Jeremy asked. Taking his mind off himself and focusing on Laluna further decreased the tension he wanted to shed.

"Oh, things have been good here. Peruma had a wonderful party and learned his lessons from previous parties. All were welcomed, and all went well."

"Ah, that's good for him! I'm glad he's doing well

and that it was successful."

"Now, it seems to me that you returned to your community with hopes to make a difference. Is that true?"

"Yes, but…"

"It's OK. Let's take this one step at a time. It sounds like you made a wise choice with the book. I heard you say that you want others to find their way, find their own journey. Is that right?"

"Yes, I remembered those creatures in the labyrinth. When I solved it for them, things didn't go so well. I felt that explaining everything I knew in the book would deny anyone who read it the experience of being here. I just wanted to encourage them to leave the community and explore on their own."

"Sounds like a truly wise approach. It seems you might have discovered that being someone you aren't or showing up to others as someone you truly aren't inside has a very real and negative impact. Is that true as well?"

"Yes, I got this job because I wanted the money, so I might have used what I learned on my journey to convince them I was more than I was, I guess. I feel so stressed and horrible inside when I'm there. In fact, I feel that I tried to be more of the person I wanted to be rather than the person I am. Does that make sense?"

"It does indeed. Those Core Disharmonies are disastrous in our lives."

"Core Disharmonies? What are those?"

"That's the name for those inner disconnections we talked about. Remember the masks that the feldorians wore? We so desperately try to represent ourselves in ways that don't align with who we are inside. Sometimes it's because it is who we want to be, and sometimes it is simply who we want others to think we are. But, in either case, that inner tension, or those inner disconnects, are the Core Disharmonies within. They are the seeds of the negative patterns we live. I'm so glad you recognize that now, my friend."

"How do you fix those?" Jeremy asked.

"It is all about continuing to learn who you are inside, truly who you are. It is ensuring that who you are inside is how you show up with others. You have just started the journey of discovering your true essence, my friend. Gaining clarity of what your mental core contains and starting the process of healing and strengthening it. Teaching what's within how you want to respond to your life takes time. It takes time to replace the patterns of responses in your memory with ones that will drive responses aligned with your authentic self. You have come so far, but you haven't come this far to only come this far."

They arrived at Fujala. The village was bustling with activity.

"What do you see here, my friend?" Laluna asked.

"Um, a lot of different characters living their lives." Jeremy replied.

"Sure, but how are they living their lives?"

"I'm not sure what you mean."

"In harmony with one another, that's how they are living their lives. Do you see how they are encouraging one another? Do you see how they help one another?"

Jeremy started to pay attention to what was happening. She was right. There was a symbiosis between everyone there. One was helping another. One encouraged another. Everyone had their role and fit that role perfectly. It was busy but peaceful at the same time. Jeremy didn't sense any tension around him.

"So, much in life is about whom you surround yourself with. It is about association." Laluna said.

"What you feed what's within is served back to you," Jeremy said.

Laluna looked at her companion with admiration. "Exactly!" she said.

"That's what I felt in my community. I could feel the negativity infiltrate me. I could feel the Reactors' reactions filling me from within, and it was coming right back out at them."

"It is so difficult to stay true to the path that has just begun when you haven't allowed time for it to truly take hold of you."

"Like Straggert and the gold?"

"Yes, my friend. We have to ask ourselves those difficult questions when others want to distract us from the path we are on. We have to ask ourselves if what we are about to do will bring us closer or further away from our defined success. And, if we continually expose ourselves to the negative, then the negative will dominate what's within."

"Forever? Is there hope to be immune in some way?"

"I wouldn't say immune, but the stronger your mental core is, the harder it is to penetrate it."

"Like the diggits, over time, they were able to only accept what was good, only what they wanted. The rest remained outside of themselves."

"Exactly! The stronger and healthier your mental core is, the more you resolve those core disharmonies, the more resilient you become. The more you practice responding by your design, the more the patterns in your memory will be positive, the more of what comes up from within is aligned with the healthy parts of who you are. The combination is then positive plus positive driving positive responses and outcomes. You can then withstand the challenges and add value to difficult situations and people without risk to yourself."

"But what do I do in the meantime? I can't be there, but that's where I live. What should I do?"

"Change can evoke fear. We fear the unknown, don't we?"

"I guess. My community has been all I've known besides the little time I've spent here, but now since I've been here, I just can't live there anymore."

"There are times in our lives we have to jump first and hope our wings will catch the breeze, and there are times that what seems like massive action can be taken in small steps. A plan is formed with the end in mind, and you prepare to be agile as you go."

"So, the end in mind is how I want to live my life. I don't have to know all the details, but I can take some small steps to see how it goes. I can then learn, adapt, and improve as things happen. Be emotionally and intellectually agile. Is that right?"

"Well said, my friend. What are some steps you can take? What are some questions that you can answer right now?"

"Well, I saved money. I wanted to move out again. I was always told, 'once a failure, always a failure,' but I know that's not true now. Just because I failed to stay moved out doesn't mean I can't try, I mean, do it again."

"That sounds very promising. What other

questions come to mind?"

"Um, I'd need to find a place to live. I'd need to find a place to live here," Jeremy said with excitement building in his voice. "But where, and what about a job? Oh, maybe this is too much. Maybe…"

Jeremy's anxiety started to build, although the answers to his questions were readily available.

"Remember, associations are important," Laluna said. "You are not alone here, right?"

"Oh, right. Do you have an idea on where I can stay or what I can do?" Jeremy felt his anxiety recede from Laluna's reassuring voice.

"As a matter of fact, I do! Peruma needs help in his shop, and he has that extra room. It would be a good start for you. What do you think?"

"Oh, wow! Yeah, that sounds great! I don't know what help he needs, but I can learn, right? I've done harder things."

"What a wonderful phrase indeed. Can you repeat that?"

"I said, I've done harder things."

"What does that mean to you? How does saying that make you feel?"

"It means I believe in myself now. You said that everything starts with a belief. We have to believe in ourselves to live the life we want, to live an Optimal Life. I've come a long way. I've done hard things recently, and I'm here, standing tall, ready to do more. I know that I can face things now, and I'll be OK. You said that problems are just opportunities, and fear is stories we tell ourselves. I have found that to be true for me now. It is my story to tell, so I can tell whatever one I want. I might as well make it positive. If I imagine the negative, what's within focuses on finding the negative. So, I'm going to imagine the positive. I've done harder things before, so I'll be OK."

"I believe in you too, my friend Jeremy. You have done hard things, and you have come so far. This is the start of a new life for you. Each moment you have can be a new start. Isn't that wonderful about life? We can always draw our line, step over it, and move forward positively. There's a choice in each moment, driven by the story you mentioned and what we've instructed what's within to give back to us. You have learned about yourself and will continue to explore who you truly are so you show up with intention in your life. Success isn't a destination. It is a process. Living your Optimal Life is to live with that intention and to add value to others, as you have discovered."

Jeremy's mind went to the young woman in the library. He wondered if she had decided to leave the community. He wondered if she would complete her journey or stop short of her success. He wondered how the others that came before were doing. He wondered if he could help them. Maybe that's what his purposeful meaning was all about! Maybe that could be living his Optimal Life.

"I'm so thankful for you, Laluna. I want to add value to others and I want to help my community. I know I can't live there right now. It is too difficult to live there and continue my internal journey, but maybe I could help those who decide to leave? Maybe I could encourage others to take their journey. Maybe I could find those that made their attempts and encourage them to make another. What do you think?"

"What do you think?" Laluna asked.

"I think that's it! I will live with Peruma if he'll have me. I'll work in his shop to make money. And I will spend my time learning more, growing more, and doing so by helping others to do the same. May I join you at times if you find another leaving my old community?"

"Why, I would love to have you! What a team we've made, and what a team we will make."

Just then, they heard a chime. It sung from nearby and from the direction Jeremy had just come.

"That might be the friend you just mentioned now."

"What was that sound? Is that how you know someone left?"

"Indeed. Shall we?"

# IT'S NOT A MYTH

Jeremy bounded up the stairs of his mom and dad's house, excited to share the good news. After a brief knock he burst through the door.

"Dad? Dad? You here?"

"God, Jeremy," his mother said. "Why the hell are you shouting? You can let me know when you're coming. You know you don't live here anymore."

"Hi mom. It's good to see you," Jeremy said. He hugged and kissed her.

"None of that, Jeremy. Oh, what's this? Another one of those evil texts you're spreading around?"

"If you mean amazing books with empowering and incredible information that is changing people's lives for the better, then yes," Jeremy replied with a smile.

"Oh, right, sure, whatever. Your dad is upstairs in his office."

Jeremy's mom hadn't quite made the turnaround that his dad had. It had been more than two years since Jeremy's original journey that led him to discover what living an Optimal Life was all about.

Jeremy wanted to think that just by being himself, living with purposeful meaning, and showing up authentically around his mom, she would change for the better just a bit.

But his dad?

"Hey old man," Jeremy said when he entered his father's office. His father sat at his desk.

"Who are you calling old?" his father replied, laughing and looking up from his computer. "Oh, is that another book?"

"Yeah, it's amazing how many we have now from so many contributors. So many want to tell their stories after they've taken their journeys, and so many from the villages along the journey's path want to provide their insights as well—diggits, feldorians, even atometes. Our new section in the library is really growing, and I've added each book to the community center as well."

His dad stood up tall, having shed his bag of rocks quite some time ago. He had been working on his own book for the last few weeks, telling the story of his travels. He gave Jeremy a big hug.

"I'm proud of you, son. You've done so much in such a short time."

Jeremy's mother walked into the office. "Oh, you two knock it off" she said. I made some snacks. They're downstairs on the table. And no noggy Jeremy." She smiled.

"She's coming along, son. She still struggles, but I think she was flipping through one of the books I brought home. It might be enough to inspire her to maybe at least visit your community center on the other side of the wall. Wouldn't that be great?"

"It would, Dad. I believe she'll make it there in her own time."

They headed downstairs together. Jeremy grabbed a snack and headed toward the door.

"I'll leave this here for you, Dad, but I have to get going to the library to drop the rest of the copies off and get back to the community center. Maybe you can come by later?"

"Sure. Maybe your mom can come with me," Jeremy's father replied, elevating his voice enough so Jeremy's mother could hear.

"Ha! Fat chance!" was her only reply.

Jeremy found his mother on his way out and embraced her tightly. "Bye mom! I love you."

She patted him on the back. Jeremy felt a relaxed feeling come over her briefly. He smiled, released her, and headed out the door.

He jumped in his car and drove to the library. He noticed workers removing the plaques that held the town mantras. The community's leaders finally agreed, after Jeremy's and others' tireless efforts, that those mantras shouldn't be part of this community any longer. Sure, there were protests, but things have shifted since the decision was made, and the idea of moving beyond those concepts is growing in support.

Things were going so well. Peruma asked Jeremy to be a partner in his business, which Jeremy gladly accepted. He found a great place to live on his own in Fujala, and then there was Sara. He couldn't wait to get back to see her. Hopefully, she was at the community center setting up for tonight's event with Laluna.

He arrived at the school and headed straight to the library.

"Another one already?" Ms. Goldston greeted Jeremy with surprise.

"Yes, indeed! I think we are going to be the biggest section in this library, eventually."

"I have no doubt you will be. Go ahead and leave them on the desk here. I'll put them on the shelves."

Ms. Goldston had been such a joy to work with in recent times. She originally wasn't happy about Jeremy convincing the school to remove the original book from the mythology section. She thought, as well as others, that's where it belonged. It took time and his own book to convince them that living a better life isn't the stuff of myth, but very much real and attainable for anyone that makes the decision to take action.

Most of the school's teachers and administrators had taken his suggestion to venture beyond the wall of the community. Their respective transformations were incredible, and this was a key that unlocked the rest of the community. Having the elites promote the idea of living an Optimal Life made it much easier for the message to be heard. It also allowed those who had traveled before Jeremy to reveal themselves. What a wonderful experience for all of them to meet and compare stories! It inspired Jeremy to build his community center. It was amazing to have a place just beyond the beautiful archway that now connected the two worlds on both sides of the wall.

Jeremy stopped briefly on his way out of the library to see all the books in the new section. He loved the title, "Your Optimal Life." The shelves were filled with stories of so many from this community taking their journeys and those that provided the journey to others. The breadth and depth of the amazing content provided in those pages far exceeded what he provided in his single book.

He thought back to the decision to not fill in the book that started it all. It was the right choice. He wasn't ready at the time. He had gained so much more knowledge and applied experiences that he had in that moment and is still learning as he goes. He knows life is a continued process of learning from others. He couldn't wait to write more books as time went on to contribute to changing the world one reader at a time. He was outspoken in his community that reading was one thing, but taking action, getting out and experiencing the world was the way to ensure true and lasting change. That only through self-exploration and taking one's personal journey can one live their Optimal Life.

He headed out of the library and enjoyed seeing and hearing the sounds of change throughout the hallways. It was such a far cry from how things were just a couple of years ago.

He quickly made his way back to his car. There was still much to do before tonight's event. He was excited to have his first of many social gatherings where he could pull everyone together that wanted to share their respective stories of transformation. There would be food, music, and fun, along with stories of inspiration.

He passed through the beautiful archway that was created just a few months ago. He couldn't imagine the wall being as impenetrable as it used to be, opening only to a select few. Now, anyone that wanted to could leave, return, and leave again. Building his community center just beyond the transitions of the two communities made sense. That way, there was a place to go to welcome new adventurers.

He parked, jumped out of the car, and headed inside the community center, excited to see his love, Sara. He knew she'd be there with Laluna and Peruma, helping them set up for tonight's event.

"Hey, everyone! How are things going?" Jeremy asked. "I just dropped off the latest book to the library."

"Oh, my friend, so good to have you back. What do you think?" Laluna asked, waving her hand across the room where the gathering would take place.

"Wow! This is amazing! This is going to be an incredible evening. Thank you so much for all your efforts, and of course, thanks to you, my love." Jeremy said, embracing Sara.

"It really is a big night for all of us," Sara said. "We've come so far since this place was built. I'm so thankful for you, Jeremy. I think back to the moment in the library when you encouraged me to read that book. It seems like a lifetime ago. The words in the book inspired me to take my journey and with you and Laluna as my guide, it led me to live a life beyond what I could have imagined, my Optimal Life."

"I'm proud of you, my love," Jeremy replied with a tear in his eye. "I'm proud of all of us."

They had truly come far. To think, a defiant beginning, a rebellious act to go against the norms created an entire movement. Small decisions and small actions created momentum that created change in an entire community. Purposeful meaning, the intended value of one's life, is to add value to others. There's no way to know how a single action can cascade forward.

Jeremy made the decision to change his life. To embrace the challenges, problems, and momentary failures. To lean into discomfort, knowing that only by pushing past imagined limits could he realize growth. He embraced the virtues of courage, resilience, and compassion to stop breathing life into his past. He started to live intentionally by preparing to respond to his life and actually responding according to his design—not by others' imposition. He realized what living an Optimal Life was. He accepted the help of another, Laluna, who empowered him on his journey. He was so thankful for who she was in his life, a true friend. He came to fully appreciate what an Optimal Life truly meant as he helped Sara to realize the same. She's now the love of his life. The first person he helped on their journey became his partner in life. That's for another tale.

Take your personal journey to living your Optimal Life.
Visit https://mycoreinsights.com to get started.


Join the conversation at
https://themythoflivingbetter.com.

Made in the USA
Monee, IL
27 February 2022